I Escaped the Gold Rush Fever

A Gold Rush Survival Story

SD Brown

Scott Peters

I Escaped The Gold Rush Fever (I Escaped #11)

ISBN: 978-1-951019-33-4 (Hardcover)

ISBN: 978-1-951019-32-7 (Paperback)

Cover design by Susan Wyshynski

Best Day Books For Young Readers

ONE

The Klamath River, California
August 1852

Pale moonlight filtered through the madrone tree's gnarled branches. Crouched in the shadows, fourteen-year-old Amelia Hudson Taylor had just enough light to recognize the figure at her feet. It was Ned Pepper, the Indian boy from a downriver nation. He lay on his side, gagged and hogtied.

How had this happened?

Amelia, or *Hudson* as everyone called her, knelt and whispered, "Do you have a knife?"

Unable to answer, Ned wriggled onto his side and glanced down at his pants.

"Front pocket?" Hudson whispered.

He nodded.

The knife was an obsidian blade—no handle—and razor-sharp. Hudson sawed through the heavy hemp rope. She nicked her fingers, winced, and kept sawing.

Finally free, Ned ripped off the gag. "How many?" he whispered into her ear. "White men?"

"At least three."

"More will come. Follow me."

Hudson grabbed his arm. "I heard them talking. They're going to burn the village at first light."

"Before long, sun rays will come," he said. "We must move like the raccoon. Low and silent."

The two teens reached the big rock at the river's edge where Ned had beached his dugout-canoe. To the east, an ominous hint of gray crept into the sky. Time was running out for the village.

"Wait here," Ned said. "I will warn them."

"I tried," Hudson said. "They're still chanting over my father. They wouldn't listen."

"They will listen to me." He got to his feet.

Hudson rose, too.

"No," he said, "you wait here."

"You're not my father. You can't tell me what to do. Father is trapped in the sweathouse. He's hurt and needs my help. I'm going with you, whether you like it or not."

The boy frowned, and she followed him up the rocky bank.

Crouched low, Hudson slipped, releasing a clatter of pebbles. Startled birds squawked. Wings beat the air, and a murder of crows burst into flight.

Ned turned and glared, shaking his head and tapping his finger to his lips.

She mouthed, "Sorry."

Ned pointed to her, walked his fingers up his arm, and then pointed to the big rock.

What? Was he ordering her to go back and wait?

Hudson shook her head. No way. Her father needed her. She wasn't some helpless girl.

Ned grabbed her arm and whispered, "Go. Wait."

"No," she hissed, jerking free. She hardly knew this boy. They'd met only a few days ago. There was no way she'd trust him with her father's life. "I'm coming with you."

He gave her a long hard look.

"And stop acting like I'm a girl. I may not be Indian, and I may be smaller, but who just rescued who? Besides we're almost the same age."

A gunshot broke the deadly calm.

Hudson flinched and dropped to the ground.

A woman screamed.

Eerie silence followed. The only noise was the hammering of Hudson's heart, pounding like a drum warning of impending doom.

Two

Five Days Earlier

Amelia Hudson Taylor, frequently called young lady by her strict domineering aunt, had run away from San Francisco three weeks earlier. To cover her tracks, she'd disguised herself as a boy and used her middle name. Hudson. She liked the sound of it; the name suited her just fine.

Hudson had traveled for long, weary days, getting through by hiding, trickery, and the skin of her teeth. She had finally arrived at the remote Klamath River Gold Strike in Northern California.

Now came the tricky part: Hudson had to find her estranged father, convince him she was his daughter, and persuade him to let her live with him.

She looked down from the trail she'd followed from Union on the coast. Trails framed the river, running parallel on each side. Both were up high, well above the winter flood-line.

Her eyes scanned the river bar. This section of the river was long and wide. She could see a quarter of a mile in each direction. The miner's settlement was a hodgepodge of makeshift tents and campsites scattered throughout the trees and brush that overlooked the river's north side.

As for the shining Klamath River, its shores were crammed with at least a hundred or more men. They crouched along both edges. Dark trails of muddy water ran from their gold pans and bled downstream.

The miners all wore the same sturdy dungarees with shirtsleeves rolled up to their elbows. Most wore crumpled, wide-brimmed hats. It was hard to tell one from the other.

Which man was her father?

Hoisting her travel pack, she started down the path toward the river. A three-minute scramble, and she reached the rocky bar edging the water. Just ahead, a big, red-haired man squatted over a gold pan. A scrawny black mule stood next to him, hobbled so it couldn't wander away. White scars, and a few fresh red ones, traced patterns over its face and back.

Seeing the poor creature with its soft brown eyes made Hudson wince.

"Excuse me?" Hudson said, taking a tentative step toward the man. "Do you know Miles Taylor?"

The red-haired miner didn't look up. He grabbed a huge handful of dirt from a bucket and dumped it into his gold pan.

"Excuse me? Sir? Can you help me? I'm looking for my father."

No answer. Not even a grunt.

He dipped the edge of his gold pan into the river. Swirling the pan to mix the water with the dirt, the contents turned brown. He poured off the excess and dipped three more times until the dirt washed away, leaving just the gravel and rocks.

"Sir?"

Why was he ignoring her? Maybe he was deaf.

She leaned closer and raised her voice. "Miles Taylor. He's my father. I need to find him."

The man swore and dumped the contents of his gold pan into the river.

He stood, hoisting his pick, and shot her a feverish glare. "Don't know. Don't care."

He spit a stream of tobacco juice onto the gray gravel. The heat dried it almost on contact, and, for a second, it looked like blood splatters. "Get lost. Quit bothering me, boy. Or you'll get a beating like old Blackie here."

Hearing its name, the poor mule brayed and lowered its head as if in fear.

The miner picked up a fist-sized rock and flung it at her. She side-jumped, and it clipped her shoulder—sharp and painful.

Hudson backed away, thankful when his glare returned to his gold pan. She beat a hasty retreat, tripping over uneven gravel the size of baseballs.

Panting, she bent double to catch her breath. Finding her father would be tougher than she thought. She bit her lip. Hopefully, he wasn't like the red-headed miner.

She rubbed her shoulder; it felt bruised and hot. Maybe even a little swollen.

"You should avoid Red Duncan," said a voice behind her. "He is a bad man."

Hudson spun around and gulped.

She stood face-to-face with an Indian boy. Even though he was taller, he looked about her age—fifteen or sixteen. His hair was tied back like a girl's in a ponytail. Like Hudson, he wore canvas dungarees, but that was all he wore. No shirt. No shoes. She'd never seen anyone half-dressed walking around in public.

She couldn't help it; she grinned. Aunt Gertrude would have been scandalized.

"You are asking about Mr. Miles Taylor?" the boy said. "I know Mr. Taylor. Come, I will take you to him."

This boy was a stranger. He might be just as dangerous as the miner.

"That's okay. Just tell me where to find him," she said.

"It is easier to take you."

Forcing a smile, she said, "But I don't know you."

"I'm Ned. Ned Pepper."

THREE

Ned did as he promised. He delivered her to her father.

"Mr. Taylor, here is your child," Ned said and left.

Hudson locked eyes with the father she'd never met. It was almost like looking into a mirror, except he was older and a man. He had the same shaped mouth, the same hazel eyes, and the same unruly curly hair.

Oh, please be glad I've come. Be the father I've imagined. Let me stay.

Her father stared at her with a look that could only be described as shock. And then, confusion. He shook his head as if to refocus his vision. A shadow passed over him, and his face grew grim.

"Father?" she said.

"You don't belong here." He sounded angry. "This is no place for a girl. Why are you here?"

"I came to find you."

"Go home."

"I can't go back to San Francisco. I won't," she said.

A frown creased the corners of his mouth.

"Please?" she said. "You don't know what it was like living with Aunt Gertrude."

"I'm sure it was fine."

"Let me show you."

Hudson slipped the suspenders from her shoulders and let them dangle at her waist. She held up her oversized baggy boy-pants with her left hand. Turning, she pulled up the back of her rough cotton shirt for him to see the scars that zigzagged across her skin.

She heard her father's sharp intake of breath.

"Everything I did was wrong." She fingered a two-inch raised patch of scar tissue in the center of her back. She knew it looked pink and ragged. "Aunt said it would remind me to be obedient."

At this, her father's frown deepened.

Hudson pointed at two more. "These stripes are for the day I snuck food scraps to a beggar." She turned and tucked the shirttail back into the pants. "If you ever loved Mother, you'll let me stay. I won't be a bother. I promise."

He stared up into the cloudless blue sky as if it would make her disappear.

Hudson added, "I'll work hard. And I can cook a little."

They eyed each other for a long moment.

"Why did you feed the beggar?" he asked.

"Because he was hungry."

"I see," he said, without any hint of a smile. He sighed, his face softening. "You can stay under three conditions."

"I agree," Hudson blurted.

He held up his hand. "You haven't heard my conditions. Only a fool agrees to the unknown." He bent until their noses were just inches apart. "Are you a fool?"

"I . . ." Hudson shrugged and stepped back. Why had her mother married this man? He seemed so unfeeling. So stern. "I hope not."

"Good." He held up his index finger. "One. You will work as hard as a real boy."

"I will."

"How old are you?"

"Almost fifteen," she whispered, thinking he should have at least remembered her birth year.

"You're small and can pass for younger. Let's say twelve." He held up a second finger. "Two, you will do as I say. Even if I decide to send you back to live with Gertrude."

Hudson nodded, crossing her fingers behind her back. She'd rather die than return.

"And three." A third finger went up. "You are a boy. Hud. Don't forget it."

"I won't." It sounded easy. After all, pretending to be a boy had gotten her this far.

She wouldn't miss the endless layers of clothing her aunt had insisted proper young ladies wore. The mid-calf skirts and crinoline petticoats. The ankle-length pantalets and long-sleeved dresses buttoned to the neck. The obligatory pinafore apron to keep the dress looking new for as long as possible.

It didn't matter what you were doing or how hot it was. In Aunt Gertrude's house, you dressed properly. You acted like her version of a young lady. Were obedient. A slave to her every whim.

The last straw was forcing Hudson to accept a proposal of marriage from the son of the largest mercantile owner—Luther Albert Banks. He was mean, rude, and a disgusting pig.

She'd rather die than marry him.

Hudson didn't tell her father this because he might agree with her aunt.

She tucked in her shirt.

As long as she didn't mess up, she was here to stay.

Four

Hudson spent a fitful and sleepless night, worried he'd send her back. But the following day, he put her to work. She was glad; no matter how hard the job, she'd give it her best. She was never—ever—returning to Aunt Gertrude's. Or worse, forced into marriage with Luther Albert Banks.

Hudson struggled under the weight of two twenty-five-pound buckets filled with dirt and rock. Someone had replaced the bucket's original wire handles with rope; the sisal cord cut into the fresh blisters on her palms.

Adding to her discomfort, the miner's pick strapped to her back dug into the tender flesh of her shoulders, rubbing against the old scar tissue.

Gritting her teeth, her breath came hard. No matter what it took, she refused to give up.

Sweat prickled Hudson's skin and streamed down her neck. If only it wasn't so hot. It must be a hundred degrees. In San Francisco, the fog rolled in and kept things cool. But here, the relentless sun beat down, even in the shade.

Hudson set the buckets down, flexed her fingers, and breathed deep. She finger-combed her auburn hair. Even short, it preferred tangles to curls.

Humph. Complaining solved nothing. At least the forest smelled sweet. Plus, sweat and blisters trumped being beat with a hairbrush.

After stretching her back, she smiled. She'd solve two problems with one solution.

She unstrapped the miner's pick and slipped the bucket handles onto either end. Then she hefted the pick to her shoulder. One bucket dangled in front and the other behind. They were still heavy, but at least it gave her blisters a rest.

Hud continued down the trail. Tall fir and pine trees reached for the sky. Bent double under the weight, she wound in and out of their shadows, following the narrow path.

This was her twelfth trip from her father's secret dig-site to the river. She'd bring him the dirt and he'd process it, sifting and cleaning it and hoping for a nugget of gold. As far as Hudson could tell, her father's secret dig-site was not going to be a lucky strike. So far, nothing had panned out.

The Klamath River's rushing water hummed on the breeze. Almost there—just one last twist in the path, and she could rest.

Her stomach growled. Hopefully, Father was ready for a lunch break.

A loud rustle sounded in the brush. She gulped, remembering her father's warning about bears.

She thought he'd been kidding. Picking up her pace, she shouted, "Go away, bear. I'm too tough to be a tasty morsel."

Grrrrrrrrrr.

It *was* a bear! Hudson ran, forgetting her father's instructions to freeze, face the animal, and raise her hands.

The growls grew louder. She put on a burst of speed, the buckets swinging wildly as she slipped and slid over the rough trail.

Grrrrrrrrrr.

She glanced back. A stand of huckleberry bushes shook violently.

Panic pushed her into overdrive. The buckets slammed her chest and back, the pick handle pressing deeper into one shoulder. Ragged gasps tore from her lungs.

A loud whistle split the air followed by a loud, "Ha, ha, ha!"

She stumbled, sending the buckets flying, and went down hard. A rock stabbed her left shoulder. Panting, she rolled onto her side and grabbed a half-rotten tree limb from the ground.

Armed, she scrabbled to her knees and used the branch to pry herself upward. Halfway to her feet, the stick cracked and broke.

She teetered but managed to remain upright, still clutching the short half. Stabbing the air, she yelled, "Whoever you are, you're not funny."

Her eyes darted to where the buckets landed. Miraculously, they both stood upright.

"Grrrrrrrrrr!" Jason Brancet, the only boy in the miner's camp, lumbered toward Hud.

Her father had pointed him out the night before. He'd warned that both Jason and his stepfather—the grouchy red-headed miner—were trouble.

"Jerk!" Hudson said, rubbing her shin.

Jason looked more like an orangutan than a bear with his long arms and orange-colored hair.

Jason loomed over her and growled again.

"Give it up," Hudson said, taking a step back. "You're pathetic. You sound nothing like a bear. More like a mouse with constipation."

Jason's cheeks turned an angry shade of red. "Oh yeah? Then why'd you run? Scaredy cat. Didn't anyone ever tell you—only stupid people run from a bear!" He reached to poke her in the center of her chest.

Before he could strike, she batted away his hand. "Don't touch me. Ever."

"Oooo. I'm so scared. *Grrrrr!*" He fake-smiled, baring his dirty snaggleteeth. "How's your dad like having a feeble-minded son?"

"Maybe you should ask your stepfather," Hudson said, inching toward her fallen buckets.

"What?" he said, scratching his head like it housed a nest of fleas. "Why would I ask my stepfather? He doesn't even know your father."

She held back a giggle. Clearly, that one went right over his head.

Jason narrowed his eyes. "What's funny?"

She mentally kicked herself. There was no point in making enemies. Not when half the miners were already at odds. Even if he was a bully. She was here to work with her dad, and she wouldn't get far like this.

Swallowing her pride, she said, "Nothing. Just that your growls did almost sound real."

"Huh. Well. Yeah. There you go." He crossed his arms. "I was right."

Talk about self-centered. Jason was big, but maybe he was younger than he looked. That would explain why he acted so immature. And lacked basic hygiene.

Too bad she couldn't send him to live with Aunt Gertrude to

learn proper manners. Coughing to cover a laugh, she nodded. "Yep. Well. Got to go. My father is waiting."

"For what? You got something in here?" Jason poked into one of her buckets then raised his finger to his nose. He sniffed, smudging a grimy mustache onto his lip. "There ain't no gold in these here pails. It's just plain old stinking dirt."

She shrugged, retrieved her miner's pick, and re-strapped it to her back.

He wiped his finger on his pants. "Want to play kick the can?"

"Sorry. Can't," Hudson said.

"Well, I do." He grinned and kicked the nearest bucket. It tipped over and rolled, spilling rocks and dirt.

Hudson gritted her teeth and clenched her fists. How dare he? If she were a real boy, six inches taller and twenty pounds heavier with muscles and a big fist, then she'd show him.

But she wasn't. Hitting him would be like a gnat attacking a buffalo.

"What's a matter? Bear got your tongue? *Grrrrrrr!*" He slapped his thighs and let out a huge, gut-busting laugh.

"Quit it."

"Why? This is fun." He kicked the second bucket.

It slammed into her shin, exploding into a blast of pain. Afraid he'd see the tears blurring her vision, she stared at the ground and swiped her hand across her eyes.

She blinked and stifled a gasp.

Cradled in the black dirt, just peeking out from beneath the bucket's rim, lay a gleaming flash of gold. She snatched up the nugget.

Eureka! she thought, her mind reeling. The nugget was the size of a large chicken egg! It had to be worth a fortune.

"Hey!" growled Jason. "That's mine. Give it to me. Now."

His big hand swung at her.

FIVE

Jason's fist zoomed straight at her face. Hud dodged, and his hand plunged past her.

Panting, Hudson snatched up the empty bucket and took a shot, swinging it at him. The bucket totally missed, but at least he jumped back. Both crouched in a fighting stance, frozen and eyeing one another.

Jason's dark gaze darted to the nugget in her free hand. "Just give it to me," he said, licking his lips. "And I won't hurt you."

She dry-swallowed, shoved the nugget into her pocket. "No."

The boy might be bigger, stronger, and meaner.

But she doubted he was faster. All she needed was a head start.

Unfortunately, that looked impossible. Jason straddled the narrow path to the river like a giant, raging grizzly. It was easy to imagine his teeth sprouting into sharp fangs, ready to tear her apart. She'd never squeeze past him.

Which left only one option. Retreat into the unfamiliar woods. Run fast enough to lose him and then double back to the river bar.

He inched closer.

She swung the bucket in a wider arc—stepping back and forcing herself to breathe through her nose. Then she took another step. And a third.

Jason kept coming, his face sinister. "Give me the nugget."

"You're crazy. It's mine," Hudson said. "I found it. Not you."

"Give. Me. The. Nugget." He stretched out his hand, his eyes berserk with gold fever.

If only she could swing her pick instead of the old bucket. Talk about a pathetic weapon. But her miner's pick was strapped to her back.

Jason feinted left, then kicked high, aiming for her stomach. As his leg shot forward, he skidded on a stone and lost his balance. His arm flailed. Hudson grasped the bucket with both hands and slammed it into his gut.

Perfect shot.

"Oomph." He groaned and bent double.

Hudson took off, running for her life. Once around the bend, she found a spot where the wall of brush thinned into random clumps and slipped into the forest. Moving quickly and silently, she crept uphill.

Below, footsteps pounded along the trail.

Hud's heart slammed. He was coming—he'd see her. *Hide,* her mind screamed. But where?

To the right, a huckleberry bush sprouted from a fallen fir log. The log was small, but the brush was thick. She put on a last desperate burst of speed, dropped behind it, and hugged the ground.

The running footsteps stopped.

Had he seen her?

Fear raced along Hudson's spine. Please, God, don't let him find me.

"Hud!" called Jason. He sounded close.

She held her breath. Why had he stopped? Was he winded? Or had he spotted her footprints leaving the trail?

"Hey," he said in a loud voice. "I was kidding. Come out. We can be friends. You don't have to hide."

Hudson stayed put. He wasn't a very convincing liar.

A heavy-sounding object clunked to the ground.

"I won't hurt you. Promise." He sounded like a little boy who'd been caught with his fingers in a cookie jar. "I didn't mean to scare you."

Silence.

"I brought your other bucket. It's still full of dirt."

Hudson pushed aside a twig to make a tiny peek-hole in the thick huckleberry bush.

Jason stood with his back to her, facing toward the river. Her father's best bucket sat on the trail. The fingers of his right hand clenched and opened like a tarantula on the hunt—over and over again.

Why couldn't he just leave?

Instead, he paced, waiting. Did he think she'd forget that he'd tried to steal the nugget? Did he think she was stupid?

By the time he sauntered off, her legs had grown stiff.

Just to be safe, Hudson counted to five hundred before making her next move.

Six

Early afternoon sunlight slanted through the trees. Hudson couldn't sit there forever; her dad would be worried. He might even be mad at her for taking so long. He'd definitely be angry when he learned she'd already made an enemy.

Still, what if Jason was waiting by the river to ambush her? He wouldn't give up that gold nugget easily.

Hud sighed, realizing it'd be foolish to take the path straight to her father. That left her forging a roundabout path through the woods, even if she risked getting lost. If she brought her father the nugget, he'd be so happy he'd forget about her scuffle with Jason. He'd definitely let her stay.

Hudson glanced into the tangle of trees. It wasn't San Francisco, and the forest might not have street signs pointing the way, but if she stuck close to the river, it would eventually lead back to her father.

Hudson stood, shoved the nugget deeper in her pocket, and unstrapped the miner's pick from her back. She gripped it like a weapon. The bucket would be her shield.

Quickly, she tramped through the woods, putting more distance between her and Jason. She clambered over downed logs, climbed up and down steep hills, and shoved through thickets of brush. Hopefully, none was the poison oak that Dad had warned her about. The last thing she needed was an itchy rash.

She eyed the nearest bush. What had he said? Leaves of three, leave it be.

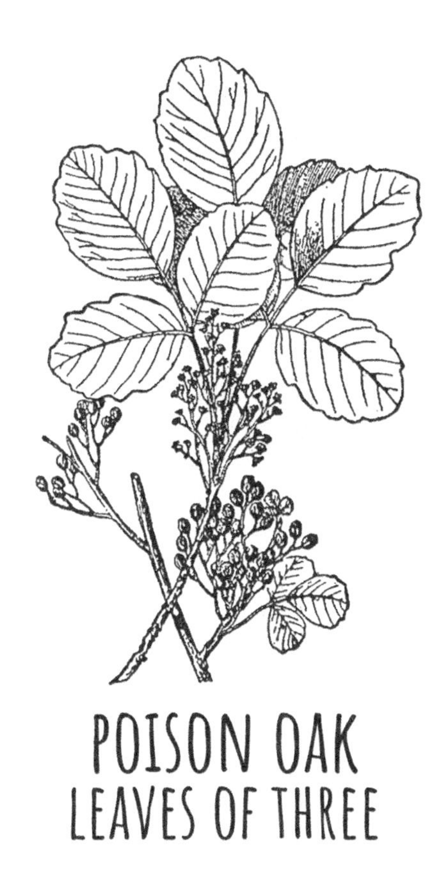

Fortunately, this bush looked safe. She kept going.

Finally, the river flashed brightly through the trees. It was time to circle back downstream. She breathed deep, and immediately wished she hadn't. Something smelled bad. She struggled to keep from gagging.

What the heck was it?

Hudson held her breath and bolted from the trees into a grassy meadow fronting the river. It should have been a peaceful view; wildflowers danced in the breeze beneath a bright blue sky. But what met her eyes was horrible.

The stench was even worse, and her hand flew to cover her nose.

Three cows lay on their sides. Angry horseflies buzzed in massive clouds around the poor beasts. The animals were clearly dead. Five red-headed vultures tore at one of the bloated carcasses. Hudson's stomach clenched.

What had happened to these poor cattle?

Voices startled her. The vultures took flight and Hudson ducked into the forest.

Two armed miners appeared, dragging an Indian boy by his long black hair. The brave looked about her age. Maybe a little older, but not much. He struggled to stay on his feet.

A third miner followed, shoving his gun into the brave's back. "Murdering savage! Killing our cows. They're worth more than three of you injuns."

Hudson stared, open-mouthed, breathing through a cupped hand. The armed men looked familiar. Maybe because they were miners.

This didn't feel right. These miners must have it wrong.

Why would the boy kill their cows unless he was starving? And that didn't make sense. He wouldn't leave the dead cows for the buzzards to eat. Or let the meat rot in the hot sun. For that matter, why kill three cows? One cow would probably feed a whole village.

An awful feeling tightened her stomach. Alarm bells rang in her head. An innocent Indian boy was about to be punished for something he didn't do.

The men shoved the boy to his knees next to one of the rotting carcasses. They pushed the boy's bruised cheek against the cow's bloated face. His dark eyes flicked to the woods, his gaze locking onto hers.

She gasped and drew back.

How had he spotted her when the others hadn't?

To her surprise, his eyes seemed to warn her. *Don't let them see you.*

She shrank lower.

"Look at our cows. Take a good, close look, boy," one miner said. "See what you gone and done, you mealy-mouthed—"

"You gonna pay," the taller man said, cutting in. "You gonna pay big time."

The boy struggled and spoke in ragged gulps. "We do not kill what belongs to another. We do not let meat rot in the sun."

"Liar!" the miner said.

"The cows, they have eaten the Klamath weed. It poisoned them," the boy said. "This is not our doing."

A pair of Indian men dressed in deerskin loincloths melted out of the trees and into view. Only Hudson saw them. Both carried rifles like the miners; they crept forward and took aim.

One Indian had long black hair, tied back and hanging almost to his waist. Three tattooed lines marked his inner forearm. He said, "Release my son."

The miners practically jumped out of their skins. They spun around. The man holding the gun jerked and fired.

The miner's shot went wide, and a branch exploded near Hudson. Bark flew in all directions. A piece hit Hudson's cheek, and she gasped.

"The next one goes in your son's head," the miner shouted.

He aimed at the boy thrashing to free himself. Two men held the youth down. They ground their feet into the boy's back and neck.

The boy's father said, "Shoot him, and we will shoot you dead."

Hudson watched the standoff in horror. There was nothing she could do. And then it happened. Guns exploded on both sides.

Time seemed to slow. Muzzles flashed, boomed, spewing the acrid scent of gunpowder. Men screamed. Bodies fell, crumpling to the ground.

Hudson felt dizzy and grabbed onto a tree to keep balance. She waited for someone to stand, to groan in agony, but no one moved.

A flush of crows rose, flapping and cawing into the air. Then the world fell silent, laced with the odor of gun smoke and the gurgle of the rushing Klamath River.

Hudson began to shiver. It was hot, but she was freezing cold. She stood on trembling legs and vomited.

Was anyone still alive? Cautiously Hudson forced her feet into the grass. She checked the boy first. It was too late.

"This was senseless. You died for nothing."

Her head clutched in her hands, she rocked back and forth on her knees and sobbed. How naïve she'd been to think Aunt Gertrude was the epitome of evil.

Tears streamed down her cheeks as she checked each man in turn. Not one had survived.

Nine bodies lay crumpled in the grass—three Indians, three miners, and three cows.

Straightening and spinning on wobbly feet, Hudson plunged across the field and ran.

Seven

Hudson leaned against a fir tree to catch her breath. The bark felt rough, but the tree's support was comforting. She'd been running forever, scrabbling through brush and climbing over fallen logs. Following the river. Using the brush as cover. Avoiding anyone who might make trouble for her. Like Jason. Or his stepfather, Red Duncan, the angry miner with the fiery hair.

The pick weighed painfully on her shoulders, but it was too valuable to abandon. That's when she realized her mistake: she'd left Father's bucket next to the poor Indian boy. Now both buckets were lost. He'd be furious.

A new worry struck. Would the miners think her father had been there? That he'd abandoned the fight and left the other miners to die? What else *could* they think?

She had to find him. He'd know what to do. She started to run.

Up ahead, a huge hill towered too steep and rocky to climb. It was time to chance exposure on the river bar. It'd be flatter, easier to walk on, and a direct route. She prayed Jason was still watching for her on the trail.

Hudson stepped onto the deserted gravel bar. A pair of mallard ducks floated in the current. There were no miners in sight.

The air was sweet, but the odor of blood and decay clung to her. She dropped to her knees and splashed water on her face and into her nostrils. The wetness felt good even though the water was murky.

She scooped up sand, scrubbed her face, rinsed, and could almost hear Aunt Gertrude's voice. "Amelia! Remember, cleanliness is next to Godliness. Therefore, dirt is next to evil."

Hudson's whispered, "No, Aunt Gertrude. Dirt has nothing to do with evil. Evil is the work of cruel, mean, and selfish people. People even worse than you."

Suddenly she felt hot, exhausted, and fearful. Her blisters had blisters.

She wanted to just sit and wait for her father to find her. To pretend that nothing bad had happened, that she could erase what she'd seen. That everything would be okay.

A horsefly landed on her hand, and she shooed it away. Fairytale daydreams didn't solve anything.

Hudson stood and brushed off her knees. It was time to get going.

The mallards quacked, beat the water with their wings, and rose into the air. They circled once and glided off, flying low over the water.

"Wait for me," Hudson called after the birds. She hurried along, ignoring the pain in her feet.

Around the next bend, miners hunched over gold pans. They were spaced at intervals along both sides of the sixty-foot-wide river. Some worked in groups. Some worked solo. All guarded their areas on the riverbank.

She finger-combed twigs, leaves, and cobwebs from her curls.

Odd. Why wasn't Father at his usual spot?

Instead, a stranger squatted there, dipping his gold pan into the river.

She thought about the abandoned bucket, recalling how his name was scratched into its side. Could someone have discovered the awful scene already?

Fear crept into her stomach.

"Father?" she whispered. "Where are you?"

Eight

Panic raced from Hudson's toenails to the tips of her curly hair. Where was her father? Miners were everywhere, but it was impossible to tell which were decent and which were evil—like Red Duncan.

This section of the Klamath River ran straight, long, and wide. Rock, sand, gravel, and boulders framed both sides. One huge white rock on her side towered high enough to hide a team of horses.

Hudson jogged past the white rock. Her stomach rumbled painfully. It was long past the mid-day meal. Wait. That's probably what happened. Tired of waiting for her to return, Father had gone back to camp for food.

She had to find him fast to explain what she'd seen and why they needed to go back for the bucket. At least if they ran onto Jason, the bully wouldn't dare try anything with her father present.

She felt for the lump of gold, glad to find it still in her pocket. Father would be furious with her, but the gold nugget would make him happy. Wouldn't it?

Not if he's implicated in murder, her mind shouted.

Red Duncan's voice startled her; she froze. He stood with his back to her, less than a dozen paces away.

"You stupid imbecile," he shouted. "Do you even know what a gold nugget looks like?"

Red Duncan was the last person she wanted to run into. The miner had to be at least six-and-half-feet tall, with over three-hundred pounds of mean muscle. His massive body blocked the identity of his latest victim. Still, Hud had a good idea who lay on the ground.

"I'm not lying. I saw it."

Hudson tiptoed backward.

"Sure you did," sneered Red. "I'm supposed to believe Miles Taylor and his boy hit the motherlode? You're nothing but a worthless lout. Lazy. Dumb. I have a half a mind to put you out of your misery."

"Look, Mr. Red," Jason's voice whined. "I got the kid's other bucket. See?"

Hudson recognized the first bucket she'd lost, sitting on the bank.

"I found another nugget in there, in the dirt," Jason said. "Not as big, but it's gold. See?"

Another gold nugget. That was hers!

Hudson had a mad impulse to run over and demand her bucket and gold.

"Keep your voice down," Red growled. "Haven't you learned nothing? Stupid boy. You don't advertise your pickings."

As if sensing her presence, the brute began to turn.

Hudson threw herself behind a redwood log and prayed. Her father had been right. He'd warned her. *Avoid that man. He's cruel. He'll kill for gold if he thinks he can get away with it.*

Sweat snaked down her neck as understanding washed over her.

Her father had downplayed the horrible truth. The Klamath Gold Rush was a place where honor and justice didn't exist.

"You find that boy," Red Duncan snarled. "Got that? Find him!"

"Yes sir," came the mumbled reply.

"Do what you have to, boy. Get me that nugget. Hear me?"

"I will."

"Find the kid. Bring me that gold. I'd hate to have to arrange three accidents." Red laughed.

"Three?" Jason's voice cracked.

"That's what I said."

"But there's only the boy and his father. That's two."

"You'll be number three if you don't deliver." Red spat a wad of chewing tobacco on the ground. "I don't leave witnesses. Got it?"

"Yeah." Jason sounded as scared as Hudson felt. "I got it."

Suddenly the gold nugget in her pocket felt like a huge weight. Red Duncan would stop at nothing to get it. And when he did, he'd kill them and keep it for himself. If he found Father's bucket, that would be the perfect excuse to string Father up as a traitor.

It was all Hudson's fault. If she'd never come, none of this would be happening.

"Now get out of here," Red barked. "Don't come back empty-handed."

Nine

Hudson waited for Red Duncan to wander away. Then, she ran. Her feet felt like they'd been filled with lead buckshot—every step sapped her hope and energy.

Red Duncan had as good as pasted targets on Hud and her father's backs.

Ahead, five men huddled by the water. They seemed excited—arms waving, fingers pointing, everyone talking at once.

Bile slithered up her throat. Were they talking about the dead men? Had they discovered father's bucket?

Giving the miners a wide berth, she rushed toward the camp.

Moments later, she reached the edge of the sprawling tent city. It wasn't a proper city like San Francisco with streets and signs. It was a haphazard maze of canvas tarps, wooden crates, and stone-circled fire pits.

Thank goodness it looked deserted.

Skirting the empty canvas huts, Hudson used the trees and bushes to navigate—left at the burnt oak tree, right at a clump of huckleberry brush, left again at the red-bark madrone tree.

Just past a thicket, their campsite squatted amongst a stand of young pine trees.

A huge sigh burst from her lungs. Father stood next to their tent.

Thank you, Lord.

"Father!"

"Hud, where have you been?" His eyes blazed.

"I—"

"It's been over two hours since you disappeared."

"I can explain," Hudson blurted. "Something's happened—"

He cut her off. "I thought we had an agreement." He untied a rope stretched between two trees. Their white tarp tent fluttered to the ground like an empty ghost. "No more excuses."

"You're taking down the tent. Are we leaving?" she said, feeling hopeful for the first time since her run-in with Jason. Leaving would solve everything. "How soon?"

"Now." He yanked the rope free, looped it on his arm, and tied it into a neat coil.

"Father." She swallowed. "I saw something—bad." The words stuck in her throat. She dry-swallowed again. "And I lost your bucket. And . . ."

"We'll deal with that later," he huffed. "Just pack the supplies. I'll get the bedding."

"But I have to tell you. It's urgent. Your name is on the bucket."

"Quit your jabbering and dilly-dallying. Get packing."

"It's important—"

He raised his hand. "Enough! Do as I say. Now." He lowered their food sack from its perch high in a tree and handed it to her.

"But—"

"Pack up, Hudson."

Hud gritted her teeth. She shoved the cast iron pan into a burlap gunnysack, and dumped everything else on top—flour, hardtack, venison jerky, tin plates, knives, forks, and cups.

"Why won't you listen?" She blinked back tears. "You're as stubborn as Aunt Gertrude."

"It's a trait you've inherited as well," he said sharply. But seeing her face, his eyes softened. "Trust me. You're not safe here."

"And neither are you. That's what I'm telling you. I saw—"

"There's no time. Tell me later." He tied the top of the gunny sack. "We have to leave before trouble starts. Indians shot three miners this morning. Killed two."

"But that's not what—"

Father talked over her. "One miner lived to tell the tale."

Wait, *one lived?* But she'd checked. Everyone was dead.

"One survived?" she asked, breathless.

"Yes. Apparently, a fourth miner was there and left him to die. The fourth man sided with the Indians."

"That's a lie," Hudson shouted.

He frowned.

Finally, she had her father's attention. "I was there. I'm the fourth miner."

A flicker of shock crossed his brow. "You?" His eyes lit with anger. "You were there? Why didn't you tell me?"

"I've been trying to. But I didn't leave the miner to die. I thought he was dead!"

Her father stared at the sky, rubbing the worry lines on his forehead. "What happened?"

The whole story came out in a rush. When it was over, their eyes locked.

"I panicked." Her voice choked. "And I left your bucket. With your name on it. Red Duncan's going to kill us. He'll say you were there, that you sided with the Indians."

He reached out and rubbed her curls. She shivered. It was the first time he'd shown any affection since she'd arrived. Then he pulled her into a tight hug and patted her back like she was a baby in need of an emotional burp.

"It's going to be okay," he said. "I'll get you to safety."

She clung to him, smelling the woodsy odor of fire on his clothes. A loud rustle sounded in the brush behind them.

Father stiffened and pushed her to the side. He pulled a pistol from his pocket and held it high.

She sucked in a breath. Had Jason given up waiting at the trailhead? Had he grown a brain and come looking for her?

"Who's there?" Father called out. "Show yourself."

Ten

A raucous donkey's bray split the silence.

The brush quivered, and Ned Pepper appeared. The unsmiling young Indian nodded to Hudson's father. Today the boy's dark hair hung loose. Other than that, Ned looked the same as when she'd met him. He was still barefoot and bare-chested.

A long-eared mule followed on his heels. One of its ears drooped forward and the other back. It was cute. It brayed again and rushed to sniff Hudson's hair.

"That tickles." She rubbed its neck. The fur felt smooth and coarse at the same time.

Father shook the boy's hand. "New plan. Red Duncan is on the warpath. It's serious, we have to leave. Now."

Ned's frown tightened. "What fire ant ran up his pants?"

"You haven't heard?" Hudson blurted. "Miners and Indians were both killed over the death of some cows. I . . ."

Father shot her a look that silenced her. She stopped petting the mule.

"Duncan's gathering a hunting party," Father said. "He plans to attack the Indian villages tonight." He frowned. "He's looking for the miner who helped the Indians."

Ned's eyes flicked to Hudson. He couldn't know she was there, could he?

The mule chose that moment to give Hudson an unexpected nudge. She stumbled.

"Chewed Ear!" Ned's hand sliced the air.

The mule hung its head like it had been slapped. Hudson took pity on the poor creature and scratched its mane. The mule snuffled.

"I'm going to Happy Camp to see Redick McKee," Father said. "He has the governor's ear."

Hudson frowned. "What good will that do? It won't stop tonight's attack."

"No. But it might stop the next one. The men are on the warpath, they won't stop at one attack." He reached into his pocket and handed Ned a handwritten note. "You head to Parker Ranch, drop my things with Gray Morgan, and give him this letter. Tell him I hope to see him within the week."

Ned nodded.

"See that my son, Hud, gets to the coast safely. Stay with him until he boards a ship bound for San Francisco."

The words were like a scatter shotgun blast to her heart.

"No," she cried, grabbing her father's arm. "Let me stay."

"That's not possible."

"Then why can't you take me to the coast? Why Ned? He's just a boy."

"Ned's a trail guide. I trust him," he said.

And not me, she thought.

"Less talk. More hustle. Grab the supplies and load up the donkey."

"Don't send me away," Hudson said. "The Klamath River is a hundred-and-eighty miles long. Can't we find another spot to pan for gold? Away from Red Duncan and his men?"

Father made no reply.

Frowning, she swallowed the urge to cry. Her dream that they'd be a family slipped away. Her clenched jaws ached.

Her father was a stubborn old mule.

Well, she could be mulish, too. She'd go. But not back to Aunt Gertrude's. She'd find a job—maybe on the docks.

The three worked in silence. Soon the supplies were tied onto the mule. Ned whistled and started off. Chewed Ear followed.

Father squeezed her shoulder and leaned closer. She waited for him to say something nice, like that he'd miss her.

"One last thing," he whispered. "Ned doesn't know you're a girl. Keep it that way."

She scowled. "I thought you trusted him?"

"Trust only goes so far. Now hurry. Red will be looking for us."

They hurried single file toward the river and Ned's canoe. She jogged to keep up.

At the gravel bar, they slowed. Here and there, angry men stood in clusters. She heard snatches of talk about the dead cows, the dead Indians, and the dead miners.

"Eyes down, Hud," Father warned. "Don't look at anyone."

"Yes, sir," she said.

It was only a matter of time before someone read the name scratched into the abandoned bucket and raised the alarm.

"Whatever happens, don't talk," he said. "Ned? Where's the canoe?"

Ned pointed past the largest mob.

Father gave a quick nod. "Flank Hud on the right. Keep the mule on your left. Be ready to run. If something happens to me, keep my boy safe."

All around, the voices grew louder, swelling like the wild river—dark, turbulent, and frothing.

ELEVEN

Hudson kept her eyes downcast but snuck quick, frightened glances. The miners gathered at the river bar seemed to have doubled. They grew rowdier, angrier. It was clear some were liquored up.

"Should we retreat?" Ned said. "Until the wolves leave the lair."

"No," Father said. "The sooner we go, the better. Follow my lead."

The mob ignored them—until one miner spotted Ned.

"Hey," the man shouted, pointing. "Ain't that thieving White Feather's brother?"

The mob swarmed like angry hornets. Every eye fastened on Ned as they closed in.

"Your brother poisoned our cows," one snarled.

"We could arrange a family reunion," shouted another, waving a bottle of whiskey. He took a swig of the firewater, licked his lips, and pulled out a pistol. "Would you like that?"

Hudson's father cleared his throat. "What's got everyone all riled up?"

"Why don't you ask your Indian friend where he was this morning?"

"I already know. I hired him to strike my camp," Father said. "Took us most of the morning."

"You sure?"

Father pointed to the loaded mule. "That's my gear. I'm heading downriver."

"What's the big hurry?" shouted another miner.

"You'll miss the hunting party," said another.

Hudson felt her father's hand on her shoulder. "Get in the canoe," he whispered.

"What about Ned? And our things?"

"Do as I say. If you can, shove the boat into the water." He pushed her toward the beached canoe and turned back to the mob.

Hud took two steps and got no further. The men attacked. She was caught in a man-stampede—jostled left and right. A fist slammed into her ribs. She crashed to her knees, and a heavy boot crushed her little finger.

Gasping, Hudson scrunched into a ball and tucked both arms over her head. Chewed Ear bolted, clanking into the trees. Father and Ned were lost to sight, trapped in the surging horde.

Dread gripped her. Dread that her father and Ned would die like the men in the field.

Please. Please, God. Make this madness stop. Please, keep Father and Ned safe.

A shotgun blasted upriver.

Hudson rolled sideways as the men scattered left and right. Rising, she blinked to clear her eyes, desperate to try and spot her father.

Men were everywhere, clamoring and shouting.

Chewed Ear stood atop the bank eating dry grass—their supplies still tied onto the donkey's back. Ned's canoe lay abandoned on a sandy patch of shore just ahead.

As for Father and Ned, they'd disappeared.

He'd come back. He just had to!

Red Duncan's voice rose above the chaos. He'd climbed atop a massive boulder and was punching a smoking shotgun into the air.

The men roared, drowning out the sound of the rushing Klamath.

Duncan fired off another blast and motioned for the men to quiet.

Silence fell. Red Duncan spoke but was too far away to understand.

Swiftly, she headed for the canoe. When Father returned, she'd be ready for him. Because he *would* return, she had to believe that! She'd get the canoe in the water first and then fetch the donkey.

Up close, the boat was huge—at least twelve feet long. It looked like a hollowed-out redwood tree that had been burned and scraped smooth.

Hudson went to the canoe's far side, using it as a block between herself and the mob. She shoved, and nothing happened. Wow. It was twice as heavy as it looked.

She planted her feet on the shore and shoved hard. Again.

It didn't budge.

Maybe if she pulled from the floating end, the buoyancy would make it lighter and easier to maneuver.

Hudson slipped off her boots, tossed them into the canoe, and rolled up her pants. The rushing water felt cool as she waded to her knees.

Red Duncan shot off another gun blast.

She held onto the canoe for balance and waded deeper. Soon, the water reached her thighs. She grabbed the stern, jumped up, and shoved it down, using all of her weight to pull the canoe into the water.

At first, nothing happened. She jumped again. Tugged harder. Leaned back farther. The next jerk made her arms feel like they were being pulled from their sockets. But it moved.

Another hard jerk and the boat floated free.

"Yes!" Finally, she'd done something right.

Hudson stood waist-high in the river, panting.

Uh oh, how was she supposed to get the donkey? The current tugged at the boat, threatening to drag it downstream.

Upriver, Red Duncan was climbing down from his rock. The mob splintered into groups. Thirty men followed Duncan toward the main camp.

She had a bad feeling about this.

A second, smaller group headed toward Hudson. To her surprise, every few yards, two or three men peeled away to return to their gold panning. Only about fifteen men remained by the time the rag-tag group reached her. They were still arguing.

Hudson spotted her father and Ned bringing up the rear. She gasped in relief. Both looked unscathed. Then she saw Ned's wrists.

They were tied with twine.

Ned kept his eyes to the ground, his feet shuffling. Hudson gulped.

Father led the boy with a rope leash—like Ned was an animal. Why would her father do such a thing? It was horrible.

"Hud," Father called out. "Push the boat back onto shore."

"But, I just—"

"Do it. Now." He shot her a dark look.

Twelve

Hudson's jaw clenched. There was no pleasing her father. Do this. Do that. Put the canoe into the river. Take it out. All her efforts had been for nothing. And now he was leading Ned like a bad dog on a leash. It was humiliating and cruel.

Father and Aunt Gertrude were cut from the same cloth after all.

She gave the boat one hard shove. It sailed forward and lodged in the sand. Her soaked pants chafed as she waded after it.

Father handed her Ned's leash and whispered, "Untie Ned."

Her eyes met his. "What's going on?"

"Do it. Now." Father hissed and then spoke loudly to the men. "This boy will be punished for what he did. After I get some work out of him."

Hudson grabbed his arm. "Why? Ned didn't do anything."

Father shrugged off her hand, whispering, "Be quick. The men might change their minds and take him."

"Oh." She shouldn't have jumped to conclusions.

To her surprise, Father bent and washed his hands in the river. Was he trying to act casual, like they weren't in a hurry to get away?

Ned held his bound hands to her, and she fumbled with the knots. Danger sparked on the breeze.

"Hurry," Father urged. "We need to skedaddle."

Hands free, Ned tied his hair back and reached into the boat for his long paddle.

"Sure you don't need help with that injun?" a miner called out. "Be glad to oblige."

"We got it," Father yelled back and waved. "My boy and I can handle one Indian youth."

The man shrugged and walked on.

"Ned's mule is over there." Hudson pointed to where Chewed Ear was munching grass. "It's still loaded with your stuff."

Ned put two fingers into his mouth and whistled three sharp blasts.

Chewed Ear raised its head.

Ned whistled again.

The mule raced down the steep bank, hit the flat ground, and trotted straight toward them. It veered to avoid two men without losing pace. The jolt sent the muslin bag that held their venison jerky flying. Hudson ran to catch the sack, but it bounced off her fingers and landed in the gravel at a stranger's feet. The stranger quickly swept it up.

"That's ours," she said.

"Was." The black-bearded man opened the sack, snagged a piece of jerky, and chewed. His white ceramic Burley pipe bounced with each bite. "Mine now and mighty fine."

"Hud," Father shouted. "Get on back."

She scowled, wishing she could call the man what he was—a no-good thief.

"What's the hurry, boy?" The man drew a flask from his pocket and took a swig. Then he held it out. "Want some? It'll put fire in your belly."

"No, thanks," she said.

The man's chin went up, and he squinted at her. It was a creepy stare. Hot shivers raced up her arms.

"How about a pull on the pipe? Got my own special blend of tobacco. Cinnamon and nutmeg."

She shook her head.

"What's your pa want with that injun boy?" he asked.

"Don't know. Didn't tell me." She shrugged. "All I know is I got to get back."

"Stop him!" someone called out. "He's the traitor. I saw him."

Hud froze.

The voice belonged to Jason Brancet. He stood on the overlook. Their eyes locked, and she gave him a quick shake of her head. This only made him smile. An awful, nasty smile. He raised one arm and pointed straight at her.

In a loud voice, Jason shouted, "That boy was the fourth miner. And here's proof. He left this bucket behind." Jason raised the bucket high.

The bottom dropped out of Hudson's stomach.

The bearded man grabbed her arm. "You killed the miners?"

"He's lying!" Hudson tried to wriggle free. "Let me go."

"That's not all," Jason yelled.

A dozen men had gathered around Jason.

"He held a gun to my head and stole my gold."

"That's a lie!" Hudson screamed, outraged.

Jason and the men streamed onto the beach like wild dogs. The bearded man's grip tightened.

"He's lying," she yelled. "Jason's the thief. Let go."

A gun blast sounded. At the canoe, her father held his pistol in the air.

"Let go of my son," he roared.

The miner's hand squeezed harder. "Shoot me and you're dead."

Hudson bit the man's wrist. He howled and let go, and she bolted.

The mob thundered after her, their shouts narrowing the gap.

She reached the canoe and jumped in. Her father took aim at the crowd.

Ned shoved the canoe into the current and clambered in over the side. The boat rocked as Ned used the long paddle to push them into the current.

The horde reached the river's edge, too late to stop them. Jason arrived last, panting and glaring at Hud.

She waved. "Bye."

The bully reached down, grabbed a baseball-sized rock, and flung it. The projectile whizzed by, landing in the water.

Jason grabbed another and sent it flying with a volley of insults.

Hudson laughed as the current carried them out of reach.

But then, to her horror, her father let out a fearsome cry and crumpled sideways. A bloodstained rock lay next to him in the canoe. He'd been hit.

"Father?" she cried.

Blood streamed down his temple, across his jaw, and soaked into his shirt.

"No," she cried. "No!"

Thirteen

Ned steered the canoe into the current.

The miner's shouts faded in the distance. Still, they had to keep moving because trails ran both sides of the river. A man in the saddle could catch up. The miners would be on the warpath.

Hudson cradled her father's head in her lap. He was unconscious, his face pale. She dipped her handkerchief into the river and wiped blood from his forehead. She rinsed the cloth and pressed it against her father's wound, trying to stop the bleeding.

Please, Lord. Don't let him die. Let him wake with nothing more than a headache.

She was afraid to the voice the words—afraid Ned would hear the sobs that threatened to tumble from her lips and realize she was a girl.

Stop this nonsense. Father needed her to be strong and focused.

Trails tracked the river. They needed to find a safe hiding place. Ned knelt at the back of the canoe, clearly worried. Suddenly he looked almost younger than her.

He gripped the paddle, using twists of his wrists to steer the canoe around boulders in the turbulent water. Hudson noticed a black line tattooed on his inner forearm. She turned away, her chest tightening at the reminder of the dead Indian in the field.

The afternoon stretched on, and still Father did not wake.

Now and then, Ned called out to shore in another language. Each time, Hudson saw no one.

"What are you saying?" she asked.

"I try to warn the Indian villages."

"Is anyone hearing you?" she said.

"I do not know."

An afternoon breeze blew as the canoe rounded a bend. The river spread out, and the current slowed to a near standstill.

Ned stowed the paddle, grabbed the long pole, and stood, shoving the pole into the water. It dug into the riverbed. He leaned onto it to push the boat through the still water. The canoe rocked gently with each forward shove.

"How is your father?" he asked.

Worried, she lifted the wadded handkerchief from the wound. "I'm not sure. His head stopped bleeding, but he hasn't awoken."

Ned stood. "That is good."

"How is that good?"

"No more blood. His sleep will allow his spirit to heal him."

She hoped Ned was right.

"When we reach the village," Ned said, "I will take him to the sweathouse. The medicine man will banish the evil spirit that is pressing your father's soul."

Hudson drew back. "No. We can't go there. The miners plan to raid the villages tonight. We'll be caught in the middle of it all."

"Do you want your father to die?"

"Staying in a village isn't safe."

"Not safe for who?"

"For anyone," she said. "Father. You. Me. The villagers. We need to warn them and keep going. Then find a place to hide until it's over."

"We have come far. It will be hard for Duncan to reach us tonight. We will be safe there."

"I wish I could believe that, but you saw how mad they were."

On shore, a gray squirrel paused to stare at Hudson.

She stared back, watching as it scampered away. The river narrowed, and the current picked up again. Ned pulled the pole from the water and stashed it in the canoe. He dropped back to his knees, taking up the paddle.

"If your father is to live, we must take him to the medicine man." He repositioned the paddle as a rudder.

"No," she said. "I told you, Red Duncan's men are coming. They'll find my father."

"He will die unless we bring him to the medicine man."

"You don't know that. He's my father. The decision's mine. Not yours."

A knot formed in Ned's jaw.

Hudson touched her father's pale cheek and whispered, "Please wake up. It's going to be okay. Don't leave me. I love you."

But he showed no sign of waking. Hud knew Ned was right; Father needed help, desperately. She felt sick. For her father, for the dead men in the field, for the innocent villagers who stood in harm's way. She never should have come to the gold fields. This was all her fault.

Ned wedged the long pole into the riverbed, stopping the canoe, and pointed at the shore. "Look. There."

Hudson squinted. She saw only the river, the brush, the rocks, and the trees. "Where? What am I looking for?"

"See the tallest tree? Look to the brush at its feet."

Hudson stared harder. It was just a ratty-looking bush, yellow and already dead.

The bush moved, and Hud gasped.

A warrior brave crouched low, clutching a spear, aiming straight at them.

The blood in her veins turned to ice.

Fourteen

Hudson stared at the warrior in terror. Then Ned raised his arms and whistled. It sounded like a blue jay's cry.

The warrior straightened. Like Ned, he was bare-chested with long dark hair. Unlike Ned, the man's hair hung loose to below his shoulders.

Ned called out in words she didn't understand.

The man nodded and jabbered a long reply.

"Is he friend or foe?" Hudson asked.

"He watches. I have told him what has happened upriver. He will send word we are coming." Ned pushed off. "We should arrive soon."

"You said that before. How much longer?"

"The river decides. You must be patient."

She puffed out her cheeks in frustration.

Her father moaned.

"Father? Can you hear me?"

His eyes moved under his pale lids. Maybe if she talked to him, he'd wake.

"We're in the canoe. Ned is taking us downriver. He says there is a medicine man who can help you heal."

Father's face gave no sign that he heard.

Hudson looked at Ned. "Can your medicine man really cure him?"

"He is skilled."

"But what about when the attack comes? What then?"

Ned's lips tightened. "It will not come tonight. You must be calm. It is all you can do. Think of something else."

"You talk like an old man," she mumbled.

He acted like he was as old as her father or something. They were the same age or close. Then she remembered the dead Indian boy. A miner had called him Ned's brother. Maybe that was why Ned was so serious. He was grieving.

"I'm sorry about your brother," she said.

Ned frowned. "I do not have a brother. Only a sister."

"Oh," she said, confused and embarrassed. She shot him another glance. If she had to trust this boy, she needed to know more about him. It was time to apply one of Aunt Gertrude's sayings: knowledge is power.

"How old are you, Ned?"

"I believe I am fifteen of your years." He traded the pole for the paddle.

"We're the same age, then."

He nodded

"Why are you helping us? Won't it anger your tribe?"

"The Karuk are not my tribe. They are upriver people. My people are Yurok, downriver people. We share the river, but we are not the same."

"Oh." She could think of nothing more to say, and Ned clearly had no interest in talking.

Hudson rinsed the rag, wrung it out, and placed it on her father's forehead. If only she could wave a magic wand and heal him. All she had were prayers, and God seemed to be ignoring them.

Why did men like Red Duncan exist? How could they kill innocent people?

She knew the answer. Her hand went to the lump in her pocket. *Gold fever.* The nugget felt twice as big and heavy as before.

Had gold lust ruled her father like it ruled the crazed miners? Is that why he'd abandoned her?

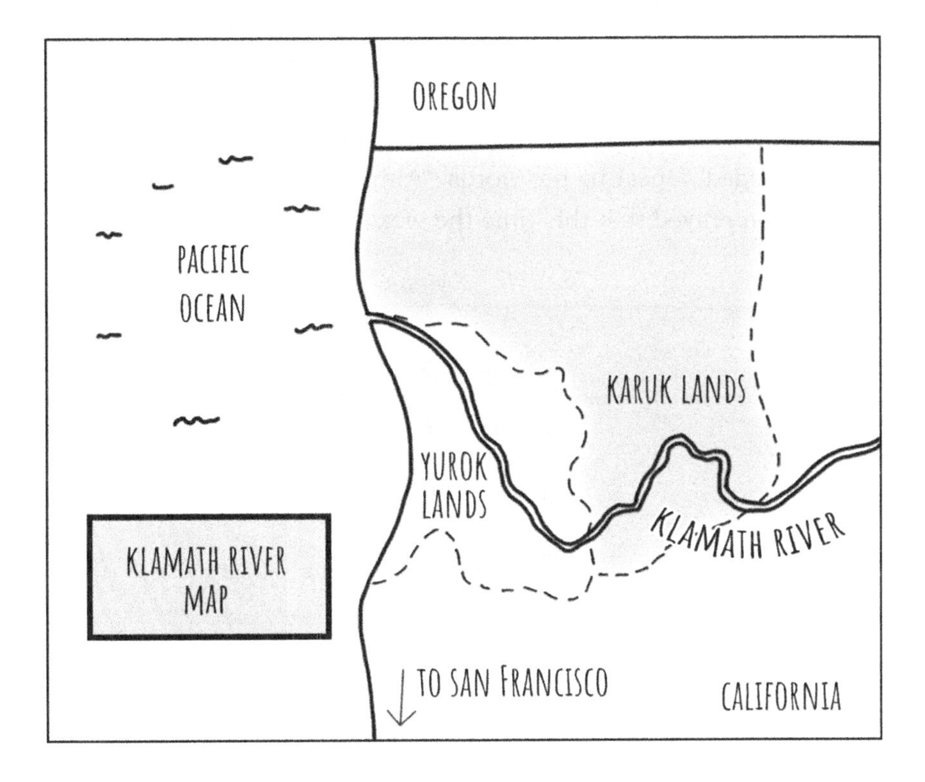

"Ned, you never answered my question. Why are you helping us?"

His gaze didn't leave the river. "Your father is not like the others."

"Did you know the Indian boy that was killed this morning?"

"You are like a blue jay. Talk. Talk. Talk. Don't you like to hear the birds sing? Or the crickets chatter?"

"I'm sorry. But don't you want revenge?"

"Revenge?" Ned's frown hardened. "You cannot change what is

past. To survive, you do not stand in the way of an enemy's arrow. There are better ways."

"What does that mean? Like wh—"

Her father's breathing suddenly grew ragged, and choking sounds came from his throat. His face turned blue-gray.

Could an unconscious person swallow their tongue and choke? Frantic, Hudson flipped him onto his side. The movement seemed to ease his breathing. He sighed and muttered in his sleep.

"Shh," she said, patting his back. "Hang on. We're almost there."

She glanced at Ned, her eyes questioning.

He nodded, repeating her words, "Almost there."

Hudson prayed that this time the words were true.

FIFTEEN

The wind picked up, drying the sweat on Hudson's forehead. The air smelled sweet, scented with forest spice and willow blooms. For a brief moment, she pretended everything was perfect.

If only daydreams could be true.

Her father stirred. "Hud?" His voice sounded thick. "Where are we?"

"You're awake," she gasped.

"Barely. What happened?"

"Ned's taking us to a village."

Father winced. "My head hurts." He struggled to sit.

Hudson gently held him down. "Don't move. You're hurt."

He blinked. "How?"

"You don't remember?" Pause. "The miners attacked us."

"Why?" Confusion flickered in his eyes. "Why would they hurt me?"

"It's a long story," Hudson began, but before she could continue, he lapsed back into unconsciousness. "No, Father. Wake up. Please, wake up."

Treetops swayed, casting shadows. They wavered like angry ancestor spirits dancing to purge the invaders who'd spoiled the Klamath with their gold lust.

"Let him rest," Ned said. "It will ease the pain."

"Stop telling me what to do. You're not in charge."

Ned might be right, but he had no right to boss her and act like he knew more than she did.

Ned looked away, his shoulders tense.

She sighed. Maybe she shouldn't have snapped at him. "Ned? Can I ask a question?"

He made a noise like a wild pig's snort.

"Is Ned Pepper your real name?"

"It is my white man name." His eyes sparkled with mischief, and for once, he looked his age. "If you were a Karuk, your name would be Kachakaâch."

"Catch-u-ca...atch? What does that mean?"

"It is your spirit animal."

"Which is?"

"You must figure that out for yourself."

"That's not fair," she muttered and shot him a dark look.

He pointed. "We are here."

She glanced ashore. "This is a village? There are only three houses. And they aren't very big."

"They are big enough."

She rolled her eyes.

The canoe slid up the sandy bank next to a massive rock monolith. They leaped out, beaching it higher.

"Stay with your father," he said. "It is best if I go alone. I must warn them that trouble flies like a snake in an eagle's beak."

This time, she agreed.

I Escaped the Gold Rush Fever

Allart van Everdingen

Sixteen

Hudson sat on the edge of the canoe kicking patterns into the sand. Her father looked almost peaceful as he slept.

Two small children peeked at her from the tall grass a dozen yards away.

What was taking Ned so long?

The village was nothing like she'd expected. Instead of a cluster of teepees, it held three houses made of split redwood planks weathered to a smoky grey. Even weirder, the houses stood only about four feet high. The doors were round holes placed at ground level, and they faced upriver.

Hudson stretched to ease her sore muscles. The two Indian boys mimicked her moves.

She waved. They waved back.

She stretched. They stretched.

She squatted. They squatted.

"Hello," she called to them.

They yelled something, laughed, and jumped up and down. Smiling, she copied their movements.

The game went on for some time. Then it suddenly stopped.

An Indian woman appeared with a basket on her back. She wore a deerskin shift, was barefoot, and had three dark-blue lines tattooed on her chin. They reminded Hudson of the tattoo on Ned's arm.

One clap of the woman's hands sent the children scooting into the nearest house.

Distraction gone, Hud's mind raced to the dangers hanging over their heads. She knelt by her father and stroked the damp hair from his forehead.

Judging by the sky, it had to be less than two hours until dark. Was it true what Ned said—that they'd traveled far enough to be safe? Her stomach churned.

Father's skin was hot.

Why was Ned wasting precious time?

The woman stood outside the nearest house. She watched Hudson, then turned and headed to the center building. That's where Ned had gone earlier. Instead of entering, the woman set her basket outside, called through the round door, and left.

A minute later, an ancient-looking man climbed out of the short house. A trail of smoke tumbled into the air, followed by Ned and two others. One carried what appeared to be a rolled-up deerskin.

The old man used a staff to stay upright, wobbling as he walked. Snow white hair fell down his back, and deep lines dug creases into his dark skin. He wore a woven basket decorated with what looked like red woodpecker feathers on his head. Around his neck dangled a pouch on a leather strip.

He was chanting. It sounded like, "Hon yee all you oh."

He must be the medicine man, she thought.

The others followed in single file. Ned brought up the rear. Unsmiling, he nodded at Hudson.

The procession stopped a few feet from the canoe. The medicine man raised his strange-looking staff. It was burned black, and an eagle feather dangled from its top.

"You must step aside," Ned said. He now wore a pouch around his neck, too.

"I'm staying with him," Hud said.

"No. You must trust the healer. We will carry your father to the sweathouse. The medicine man will banish the evil spirits that have stolen your father's health. You must wait."

She gritted her teeth, weighing her choices. It seemed she had none. Reluctantly, she stepped back. "How long will it take?"

"That is not for me to say," Ned answered.

Hud's eyes darted to the trail above. "They know the miners are on the warpath, right?"

Ned nodded.

The medicine man started to sing in a high and reedy voice. Shivers raced from her neck to her toes.

The shorter man unrolled the deerskin and laid it on the ground. The taller man had a scar on his chest. He, together with Ned, lifted her father from the canoe. They placed him on the skin.

Father groaned, and Hudson rushed forward.

"Stay out of the way," Ned ordered.

The medicine man turned and started up the trail to the sweathouse. He sang louder. Ned and the other two carried her father in the deerskin stretcher, heads bowed.

Despite Ned's orders, Hudson trailed behind. This might be Ned's world, but they were carrying her father. She wasn't leaving his side, and that was that.

She said a silent prayer. Let Father recover. Soon. Before Red Duncan attacks.

The procession reached the sweathouse. The medicine man pulled aside the animal skin door-flap that covered the round hole. He entered feet first but facing out. The men set the stretcher on the ground. They entered the house the same way, one at a time. Ned waited outside with her father.

The tall man with the scar reached out and lifted one end of the stretcher. Ned took the other end. Together they maneuvered her father into the sweathouse. Last, Ned went inside.

The deerskin door-flap dropped and blocked Hudson's view.

She rushed to push aside the animal skin. Smoky heat blasted her face, and she coughed.

Ned appeared. "Go."

"He's my father," she said. "I'm coming in."

"You are not allowed to enter."

"Why not?"

"Only men may come inside. No women. No children."

"You and I are almost the same age. We're both boys. If you can enter, why can't I?"

"You are small. You look like a child," he said and dropped the skin curtain.

It wasn't fair. Just because she was small, it didn't mean she was a child. Doubt assaulted her. What did this medicine man really know? He was no doctor! Could she trust Ned to protect her father?

Hud leaned against the rough redwood-plank wall until her shoulder went numb. She pushed away and paced. Sat. Stood. Leaned and paced. Sat again.

What was taking so long? It had been hours. Faint stars began to sparkle overhead. Danger whispered in the air.

She turned, her eyes peeled on the trail that cut along the hillside.

A hand touched her shoulder, and she jumped.

Seventeen

Panic shot up Hudson's spine.

She spun to find the woman she'd seen earlier, the one who'd called the children.

"Come with me," the woman said. "The air grows cold."

Hudson's heart slowed to a trot. "My father is inside. I can't leave him."

"Your presence does more hurt than good."

"I have to watch for Red Duncan's men. They're planning to burn the villages down."

"We are far from the miner's camp, and there are many villages along the river."

"That won't stop them. As long as we're here, you're in danger," Hudson said.

"How do you know this?"

"They'll be looking for revenge—on your people and on my father."

"We are one village of many. They can't attack every village. You need rest. And strength to help your father."

"No, I'm fine," Hudson said.

The woman gently took Hudson's arm and pulled her to the next house. "Come. Sleep. It is late."

I won't sleep Hudson thought. Not until Father and I are safely back in that canoe. Still, she allowed herself to be led to one of the short houses.

The woman spoke to someone inside and then motioned for Hudson to enter— feet first, facing out.

Hudson nodded. Backing into the house was clearly important, and she wondered what it meant. It seemed a little odd, but these people were trying to help her father, and she would respect their traditions.

Hud dropped to her knees and crawled backward into the door. Hands grabbed her legs. She started to panic. Then she realized the hands were guiding her feet onto a step.

Climbing down, her eyes adjusted to the darkness. A small fire in the room's center gave just enough light to see. She stared in awe.

The houses might look short from the outside, but inside they were tall. They'd been dug deep so that the bottom half was below ground. A wide shelf carved into the wall ran around the whole perimeter. Positioned along the ledge at intervals lay at least a dozen sleeping kids.

The woman led Hudson to her place to rest and then lay with the other women dozing on the floor. Many snored or wheezed.

Hudson rubbed her face. Maybe the raids were just a drunken man's ranting—full of talk and no action.

No, she'd never believe that.

But were all the miners bad? They couldn't be. Her dad was a miner, and he was a good man. There had to be more like him. So why were people like Red Duncan allowed to take control? Why didn't the others stop him?

She knew the answer.

Fear. Duncan was a bully of the worst kind, and he had the size and muscle to back it up. Out here in the Wild West, there was no law. Ruthless men could threaten, beat, steal, and murder without consequences.

Someone had to put a stop to Duncan's ruthless tyranny. Perhaps the man that her father had mentioned could do so. What was his name? Redick McKee. The man who had the governor's ear.

When her father awoke, they'd escape and go see McKee and tell him about the atrocities.

It had been a long day. Hud felt bruised all over. Was it only this morning she'd lost the buckets? She yawned. Just for a minute, she'd rest.

A noise jerked Hud awake. Confused, she bolted upright and realized she was in an Indian house and not a San Francisco Victorian home.

A woman snorted in her sleep. That must be what had awakened Hud. Still, fear shivered down her back. What had she been thinking coming in here?

Propelled by worry, she tiptoed through the sleeping bodies and climbed outside. Cautiously, she peered around.

The fresh night air felt good after the stuffiness inside the house. Bright stars twinkled overhead. She saw no sign of any watchmen, but then they were probably well hidden. No sounds came from the sweathouse. It seemed the whole village was dozing.

She needed to use the bathroom. Did the Indians have a designated bathroom spot? It wouldn't be in the village. She crept away from the houses, looking for a private place.

The crescent moon gave her just enough light to navigate the shadows. Hudson headed southwest, hoping she wouldn't mistake poison oak for a huckleberry bush. She took care of business and went down to the river to wash her hands. Halfway back, she heard a noise—an animal moving on the hillside?

Uneasiness crept up her throat.

Another sound. *A thud?*

Could Ned be trying to get her attention?

"Ned?" she whisper-shouted. "Are you out here?"

No answer.

Ned didn't seem the type to play games.

A whiff of cinnamon-scented pipe tobacco wound tendrils in the air. It reminded her of the black-bearded miner who'd stolen their jerky, the one with the ceramic pipe. She remembered how he'd grabbed her in his tight clutch.

The scent came again, awful and familiar.

Every hair on Hudson's neck sprang to attention.

Be silent and move fast.

Scrunching low, Hudson reached the short house undetected. She woke the English-speaking woman and whispered in her ear.

"The miners are outside."

"How do you know this?" the woman whispered.

"There's no time to explain. Get everyone out quietly. I have to find Ned and my father."

EIGHTEEN

The woman scrambled to her feet as Hudson crept outside. Clouds floated across the night sky, blotting out the moonlight. In the blackness, she sniffed, tracking the scent of the cinnamon-scented tobacco smoke. It came from up the hill, near the trail.

A thought struck. It couldn't be the angry mob Red Duncan had whipped into a frenzy. The Indians would have heard them coming from a mile away. This must be a scouting party, with the black-bearded man and one or two others.

Keeping low, she hurried to the sweathouse, pushed aside the deerskin-curtain, and hooted. Hopefully, the black-bearded miner would mistake her hoot for an owl.

A hand grabbed her wrist. "You do not belong here. Go."

"My father is—"

"Is sleeping," hissed the gruff voice.

"—in danger," Hudson whispered. "And so are you. There is a white man on the hill."

The hand tightened on her wrist.

"Warn, Ned," the voice said. "He keeps guard under the madrone tree above the river."

"You need to get everyone out, now," Hudson urged.

"There are more medicine words to be said."

"There's no time. My father's life depends on it."

"Your father's spirit depends on the words."

Hudson backed away from the door, frustrated. She had to find Ned. She only hoped the miners hadn't found him first.

The air grew suddenly cold. It must be almost dawn.

The giant madrone tree stood on the hillside, halfway between the river and the high trail. Could she reach the tree without alerting the miners? If Ned was up there, what was he doing? He had to have smelled the pipe smoke.

Hud crept from bush to bush, squinting in the darkness, praying she wouldn't be spotted. The clouds parted for a second. Five paces away, the big madrone tree's lower branches draped down to create a kind of hiding place for deer.

She scooted under the tree's covering.

"Ned?" Her soft words blended with the breeze.

Ten feet up the slope, a shadow moved.

It was a man's silhouette wearing a wide-brimmed miner's hat.

Terror trickled down her neck.

The miner carried a stick slung over one shoulder. It poked skyward.

Wait. That wasn't a stick—it was a gun! A rifle or a shotgun.

Hudson inched deeper into the leafy tree cave, her heart slamming. Through the branches, she saw the man's shadow shift. Had he heard her?

The red glow of a pipe was followed by a smoky exhalation. The man said, "Quit yer pacing, Bud. The attack's not 'till first light. You're wearing me out with yer pacing. Sit down and wait for Red's signal."

"You keep your trap shut," growled a rasping voice. "I know how to follow orders."

"How's about you check on our prize?"

"Lay off. He's not going anywhere."

Hud could make out three shadows. How many more?

And where on earth was Ned? She swallowed down an awful foreboding. Is that what they meant by their prize?

Suddenly, it all seemed impossible. She pressed her hands to her face; they were shaking. She'd tried to be brave; she'd tried to keep her chin up. She'd been running and fighting and doing her best. Now, though, the truth crashed down. They'd soon be surrounded with no way to run.

She huddled against the madrone's sturdy trunk. When her foot bumped something soft, her heart skipped.

Not a log.

Logs didn't grunt and move away.

Nineteen

Hudson had just enough light to recognize the bound and gagged figure at her feet.

Ned!

He lay on his side, hogtied, his mouth silenced with a rag. Hud shot a rapid glance at the miners. She'd found their prize. She had to free him before they came to check on him.

Hud bent close to his ear and murmured. "Got a knife?"

Ned nodded, wriggled onto his side, and gestured at his front pocket with his chin.

The knife was an obsidian blade—no handle—razor sharp. She withdrew it from its leather sheath and sawed through the heavy hemp rope. Hud nicked her fingers. Winced. Kept sawing.

Free, Ned ripped off the gag. Before he could speak, she slapped a hand over her mouth and shook her head. Then she pointed downhill, hoping he understood that they'd need to move silently.

The two teens crawled until it was safe to stand, then sprinted to the big rock at the river's edge where they'd beached Ned's dugout-canoe.

"What happened?" Hud said.

"I was foolish. I did not expect the miners to come so quickly. You were right."

He'd said she was right? Her eyes widened, but only for a moment. What did it matter, being right? They were still in trouble.

"How many men did you see?" he asked.

"At least three."

"We must hurry."

She grabbed his arm. "They're going to burn the village at first light."

He nodded. "I, too, heard them speak. Before long, sun rays will come."

As if in confirmation, an ominous hint of gray crept into the eastern sky. Time was running out.

"I tried to warn everyone," she said.

Ned nodded. "Good. Wait here."

"No, I'm not going to wait here."

"I must move like the raccoon. Swift and silent. You wait."

She could hardly believe it. She'd saved him, and now he was trying to suggest she was noisy?

"You're not my father," she sputtered. "You can't tell me what to do. Father is trapped in the sweathouse. He's hurt and needs my help. I'm going with you whether you like it or not."

The boy frowned, and she followed him up the rocky bank.

Hudson slipped, releasing a clatter of pebbles. Startled birds squawked.

Ned turned and glared.

She held her breath. Mouthed, "Sorry."

Ned held up an open palm. He pointed to her, walked his fingers up his arm, and then pointed to the big rock.

What? Was he ordering her to go back and wait?

Hudson shook her head. No way. Her father needed her. She wasn't some helpless girl.

Ned grabbed her arm. He whispered in her ear. "Go. Wait."

"No," she hissed, jerking free. She hardly knew this boy. They'd met only a few days ago. There was no way she'd trust him with her father's life.

He gave her a long hard look.

"And stop treating me like I'm a girl. I may be smaller than you but we're almost the same age."

A gunshot broke the deadly calm.

Hudson flinched and dropped to the ground.

A woman screamed.

Eerie silence followed, except for the pounding of Hudson's heart. She pushed up into a crawling position, ignoring the rocks digging into her knees. Stared at the village. Squinted.

Dark shadows slipped between the Indian houses. Shadows of men—men with guns.

Snick. Snick. Snick. Flint strikes ignited torches. They were everywhere. Suddenly the flaming sticks were flying through the air. They would burn everything to the ground. The wood houses were like tinder waiting to be lit.

Hudson bolted toward the sweathouse with one goal in mind. Saving her father.

Halfway there, the tall grass surrounding the village burst into flames. Everything would be burned to the ground. Hopefully, the women and children had fled.

The fire raced toward the sweathouse. Flames caught the edge. They licked upward, consuming the dry, weathered boards.

Heat blasted Hudson. Acrid smoke assaulted her nose, and the taste of fire filled her mouth.

"No," she cried, rushing forward.

Loud shouts and shotgun blasts pierced the air.

A body slammed her from behind. She went down—her attacker rolled onto her and trapped her. Angry tears streaked her face. She thrashed. Kicked. Bit the arm wrapped around her jaw.

To her horror, the sweathouse exploded into flames.

"Father," she screamed. "No." This couldn't be happening. She strained, desperate to see him come bursting out. To see his familiar form. The flames leaped higher. The roof collapsed with a *whoof*.

Her heart stopped. She knew he wasn't coming back to her. Ever.

Then like a pack of ravenous wolves, miners swarmed the village from all directions. Shouting curses. Shooting at anything that moved—men, dogs, women, and children.

Hudson felt numb. How had the beautiful dream of joining her father for the Klamath River Gold Rush turned out like this?

TWENTY

Ned dragged Hudson toward the river and the canoe.

"Let me go." Hudson tried to free herself from his grasp.

"Stop fighting," Ned said. "I am not the enemy."

"Father needs help." She fought back tears, refusing to accept he was dead. "I won't run away."

"Look." Ned pointed to flames high enough to singe the sky. The raging inferno had swallowed all three buildings. "Your father flies with the great spirit. We must go."

Hudson hesitated.

More gunshots rang out.

"I am going." Ned released his grip on her arm. "Stay if you want."

He pushed the canoe into the river and jumped aboard. He held it in place with the long pole. "Decide."

Ned was right. Father would want her to live. He wouldn't want her to stand there and let Red Duncan mow her down with his shotgun. She tore her eyes from the blazing sweathouse. She could almost hear his voice in her mind shouting, "Run. *Run!*"

Hudson scrambled into the water. Her foot skidded off a rock. Her arms shot out and caught the edge of the canoe. She clambered aboard and stood, staring back at the village.

Ned used the pole to push into the current.

"Look!" shouted a man from the hillside. "In the river! Two more are trying to escape."

Three men raised their guns and aimed.

"Shoot 'em!" shouted one. "Don't let them get away."

Hudson dropped to her knees. "Ned! Get down."

He dropped next to her as three rifle blasts sounded. Two bullets hit the water. One thudded into the side of the thick redwood canoe.

The canoe was tipping in the rough current. On instinct, Hudson wrapped an arm around his shoulder and rolled into the river pulling him with her.

They sputtered, coming to the surface. Using the canoe as a shield, they aimed it into the current. The canoe dragged them downriver like rag dolls.

More gun blasts—three more bullets hit the canoe. The boat rammed into a rock and careened sideways.

Hudson went under, and came up gasping. Blinded by the surging water, everything looked blurry. Frantic, her arms flailed like a spinning waterwheel.

She surfaced, gulped for air, and was dragged under again. The current sucked her to the bottom, hurling her downriver. Hudson fought but couldn't break free of the river's relentless surge. Her lungs began to ache. Tiny air bubbles escaped her lips.

Had she survived the attack on the village only to drown?

The thought made her fighting mad. Her arms churned. Her feet kicked off the bottom, and she shot to the surface. Gulping in precious air, she scanned for Ned.

The current had swept her around a rocky outcrop, out of sight of the miners. Still, she could hear gunshots. Had Ned been hit? Where was he? Then she spotted him. He floated face down, twenty yards away.

A fresh boost of energy spun her legs into action. She swam to him and, treading water, flipped him onto his back.

"You better not have drowned," she cried and slapped his face.

His eyes popped open. "A bullet came close. I cried out. Like a possum, I died and floated downstream."

"An old Indian trick?" she said, relieved he was alive.

"To survive, you must become one with nature."

"To survive, we must swim for shore," she said.

"We must swim downstream," he said. "Put distance between us and the men."

"No. You gave me a better idea. Follow me. We don't have much time." She swam toward the village side of the river.

"You are confused," he said. "We swim toward the wrong side. The crazy men will capture and kill us."

"No, they won't. I have a plan."

He scowled but followed.

There would be time to mourn later. Right now, she needed to survive. She had to get justice for her father. She had to escape.

Huge gray boulders jutted like tombstones along the bank. Reeds and big-leafed water plants grew between them. The jutting stones reminded her of a church graveyard.

They were exactly what she needed. Hudson crawled between two of the larger rocks.

"What are you doing?" Ned asked. "We must go."

She grabbed mud and moss from the river bottom and slapped it on her head. "I am becoming one with nature."

"This is not a good idea. The miners will track us. They saw us lose the canoe."

"Sit. Now. Before they come."

He sat but didn't look happy. Hudson plopped a pile of moss on his head and grabbed two big clumps of reeds. She handed one to him. "Now we are one with the river."

She put her finger to her mouth. "We wait until they grow tired."

Sliding into the water, she disappeared into the reeds.

Waiting.

Remembering.

The vision of the sweathouse in flames was seared into her eyes. Which led to grieving. For her father and what might have been. At least she didn't have to hide her tears from Ned. He couldn't see them.

The sun inched skyward until it reached high noon. They'd been submerged for hours. Hud's teeth began to chatter.

Had the miners moved on? Had the plan worked?

Just as she decided it was safe, a shadow moved to her right.

She froze, but her eyes swiveled. In her side vision, she saw the creature. It was inches from her face—a hungry-looking fox leaning down to lap the water. She gasped.

Should she freeze, fight, or flee?

Twenty-One

Terrified, Hudson sprang to her feet and shook the reeds, hissing, "Shoo! Go away."

Water droplets flew from her arms.

The mangy fox bolted off up the hill toward the trail—the trail that led back to the miner's village.

"Quiet," Ned hissed. "The fox only drinks the water. He did not come to kill." He stood, waded ashore, and started up the steep bank.

"Where are you going?" she asked, still submerged to her ankles.

"I go to look from the top."

Dragging muck, she hobbled after him. Stiff from crouching so long, her half-numb legs were slow to respond. Wet pants chafed her legs. The long soak had turned the cuts on her hands pale and puckered. Her boots squished with each step. Ned, on the other hand, sprinted upward.

When she reached the trail, Ned had disappeared.

Her mind ran wild. Had the miners captured Ned? Or had he abandoned her?

"Ned?" she called. Then, throwing caution to the wind, she shouted, "Ned!"

"Help," came a voice.

It didn't sound like Ned. But she thought she recognized that voice.

"Help," the voice cried. "I'm hurt. I can't walk."

Jason.

Warily, she stood her ground. Was this a trick? He was the one who started this nightmare. Was he pretending to sound injured so she'd come out of hiding?

"Please," Jason cried. "It hurts."

Crouching in the brush, she grimaced. Where was Ned?

"Hurry, please, oooh!" Jason said in a half-sob. "I'm under the pine tree with the dead top. Overlooking the river."

She scanned the skyline and spotted the dead treetop.

"Ned?" she called. "I wouldn't take off on a friend. Unless they deserved it."

"I'm here, Kachakaâch," Ned said in a low voice.

She jumped. "Where did you go? Why didn't you answer? And stop calling me Catch-u-ca…atch. Whatever it means."

"I look for canoe."

"Did you find it?"

Ned shook his head. "You should talk silent. It still is not safe."

Jason's voice came again. "Don't leave me." This time his whine was laced with pain, and it sounded real. "Please, Hud."

So, he knew it was her.

"It's your fault my father is dead," Hudson shouted, not caring who might hear or that the village was dangerously close. "Why should I lift a finger to help you?"

"Because your father isn't dead." Pause. "Yet." Pause. "And I know where they took him."

Hope flared in Hudson's heart. But she wasn't stupid.

"Why should I believe you?" She tried to sound like she didn't care, but she was already moving in his direction.

Ned grabbed her arm; she fought him off.

"I thought you were Red Duncan's best boy," she called.

"He left me here to die. I'm scared. I think my leg's broke."

Hudson followed the sound of Jason's pleading voice with a reluctant Ned at her heels.

"Don't trust him," Ned said.

"What if he's telling the truth?" Her voice was soft, desperate.

"I never wanted to hurt you," Jason cried. "I wanted to be friends."

She hesitated, certain that was a lie. She couldn't stop herself, though.

A squirrel scurried across the trail and up a pine tree.

Ned said, "Stay back. I will go look."

"No. It's my father. My call," she said. "I'll deal with Jason."

After a moment, Ned nodded.

Jason called, "Hurry, you can still save your father. I couldn't save mine. Red murdered him." He was blubbering now. "I saw him do it. He said he'd kill me if I told anyone. That's why he kept me close and brought me up here where I knew no one. I was like his slave. And he made me do things I didn't want to do. Like ratting on you."

The pine tree with the dead top was close. Hudson made a beeline for it. Here, so near to the village, the smell of smoldering smoke lingered from the attack.

She burst into a small clearing.

Jason lay half-propped against the trunk. Leaves and burrs clung to his orange-colored hair. Tears left streaks on his dirty skin. His right leg was twisted at an unnatural angle.

Jason had told the truth. He'd been abandoned and left to die.

She almost felt sorry for him. Then she caught sight of the charred remains of the village below. Smoke shrouds hung over the remains of the ravaged settlement. Tendrils reached skyward, wafting from the charred Indian houses.

Squeezing her eyes shut for a moment, she saw the two little children waving at her. Hudson's chest tightened. Even if they'd run into the woods, she doubted the villagers had escaped the guns and rampaging miners.

Those children had had no idea they were waving goodbye forever.

She turned hard eyes on Jason.

"Where's my father?"

TWENTY-TWO

"I'm waiting," Hudson said, staring at Jason. "Where is my father?"

"Red Duncan took him." Jason wouldn't meet her gaze. His voice sounded weak. "They're holding a trial. Tomorrow morning, Red will hang your father."

"A trial? He's not a judge. He can't do that." Hudson's heart thudded like war drums. "It's against the law."

"No one can stop Duncan."

"I will," she said.

Jason looked at her, his eyes bloodshot. "Grown men can't stop him."

Ned knelt examined Jason's leg.

"Then why did you say I could save my father? I'm not afraid of Red Duncan. Even if you are." Her heart was quaking. "I will rescue my father." She started to walk away. "Are you coming, Ned?"

"First, I must straighten his leg. So he may walk again." Ned grabbed Jason's foot and pulled.

The boy yowled.

"Now we go."

"You can't leave me," Jason blubbered. "I said I was sorry. And I am. Very sorry."

"You're sorry?" Hudson said. "Prove it. Tell us everything you know about Red Duncan."

"He's mean. Likes his whiskey. And has killed lots of men."

Hudson snorted. "Tell us something we don't know. Something that will give us an edge."

Jason winced. "He doesn't like being called Irish."

"You're wasting our time. Come on, Ned."

"Wait," Jason pleaded. "He sleeps with his shotgun." His words came out in a rush.

Hudson breathed deep. This might be useful information.

"He has a secret signal. When he puts his finger to his nose, it means no mercy." Jason's voice grew bolder. "And I know where he keeps his stash of gold. I'll tell you where it is when you come back for me."

Hudson took off at a brisk walk and called over her shoulder, "I don't want his gold. It's gold fever that's caused all this death."

"You haven't got a chance of saving your father," Jason shouted. "Duncan will kill you. Then what will I do?"

"Pray for our success," she said. "Then we can rescue you." Under her breath, "Even if you don't deserve it."

They walked in silence. Hudson led, and Ned followed.

The hot afternoon breeze dried her shirt and then her pants.

Hudson stopped counting her steps when they reached five thousand and the blisters on her feet went numb.

They were nearing the point in the trail that she traveled only days earlier when she'd arrived in search of her father. She'd dreamed of a better life. The mountains, trees, and river had seemed magical and pure. But today, she noticed the dead treetops and vultures circling on the breeze.

Her fairytale dream of a life free of Aunt Gertrude's tyranny had given her the strength to escape San Francisco. Miles Taylor had been just a name, not a face back then. He'd been a stranger, not the father she loved. He was her family, the only true family she had, the only person she could remember who really seemed to love her.

She was terrified, but she'd face her fear head-on. If she had to, she'd grab its red beard and shake it until it toppled.

That would not happen without a solid plan. Her thoughts turned to what they needed to do when they reached the miner's camp.

The sky turned to dusk, and they were still walking.

"Ned, we need to hurry. Are we close?"

He nodded.

"Good. I have a plan of attack." She told him and ended with, "Once we spy out what we're up against, we can adjust things."

"Your plan is smart. But you and I should change jobs. You rescue Chewed Ear. I will rescue your father."

"Do we always have to argue?" Hudson said. "Chewed Ear is your mule. Father is my father."

They rounded a bend, and Hudson knew where she was. They

were close, and it was time to leave the trail. They slipped into the trees and walked parallel to the path. The sky grew dark.

Ahead, the tent city was just visible. Strong winds gusted upriver and buffeted the white tents. They flapped like ghosts beneath the darkening sky.

"A storm is coming," said Ned.

"Good. It'll help hide us."

They reached the tent city. It was deserted, but the men were nearby. Loud, drunken shouts and laughter drifted on the breeze. It was time to act.

She glanced into a tent and spotted a hat. "Forgive me for stealing this," she mumbled and shoved the hat on her head.

She and Ned slipped through the shadows. The men's voices grew louder, more raucous. A flickering glow lit the misty air ahead. Then, a big bonfire came into view, burning bright on the river bar.

Hudson and Ned inched through a stand of brush.

Beyond the flames, Red Duncan sat on an eight-foot-high rock, guzzling whisky. King-like, he held his shotgun as if it were a royal scepter. Wearing a wide grin, he surveyed his subjects below—eating, drinking, fighting, laughing, yelling. There had to be at least fifty men.

So many. Too many.

Duncan took a last pull on the bottle then tossed it high in the air. At the same time, he raised his shotgun and fired. The blast shattered the glass to a roar of cheers.

"Where's Father?" Hudson whispered.

Ned pointed to a giant oak tree. It stood on a rise at some distance from the party, away from the river bar.

Sweat broke out on her forehead. "Oh no. What have they done to him?

Twenty-Three

The towering oak tree might be far from the mob, but four burly men stood guard next to it. Their prisoner was tied to the trunk.

Hudson nearly crumpled with fear.

Father!

His arms dangled, and his head lolled to the side. She was too late.

Squeezing back tears, she whispered to Ned. "Lend me your obsidian knife."

"Why? The mob will kill you," Ned said.

"Lend me your knife."

Ned growled. "We'll do this together."

"No. You find Chewed Ear."

"I'm not letting you—"

"Don't argue," Hudson said. "I have to do this."

Sending him away would get him out of danger, and she owed him that much. She knew he'd never find Chewed Ear in time. The donkey could be anywhere in the wilderness by now. But at least

Ned wouldn't be caught in the crossfire. He'd done so much to help her and Father, and this was no longer his fight.

Ned's shoulders slumped. "Kachakaâch . . ."

She met his eyes.

He said, "You have the heart of a mountain lion."

"I'm sorry for what's happened," she said.

"It's not your fault."

"Maybe, but it feels like it. I'm glad I got to know you. Tell your people that we're not all bad."

He handed her his sheathed blade, laying it gently on her open palm. He squeezed her shoulder and slipped away.

Hudson stood alone in the darkness, searching for the courage that wasn't there.

She slid the razor-sharp tool into her pants pocket. If she'd been smart, she'd have torn a strip of material to wrap a handle around one end of the blade. But what would be the point? There was no need for that now. She'd reached the end of the line.

Time to get going.

Pulling the hat low to hide her face, she moved casually and quietly toward the towering oak. Fifty yards away, she paused in the shadows to study the three guards. One was tall and lanky. A second was large and bald. The third had a black handlebar mustache. The fourth was short, with a scar running down his cheek.

The tall man said, "My turn."

To Hudson's shock, he pulled a knife from his boot, took aim flung it at her father.

Hudson sucked in her breath, helpless to stop it.

Thunk!

The knife struck the tree inches from her father's drooping head.

Yet father flinched. He flinched! Hope flickered. He was still alive.

"Missed," shouted the scarred man.

His friend leaned on a big stick and glared. "Think you can do better?"

"Watch this. I'll show you a bullseye." The man's words were slurred. He stumbled, dropped his knife. Bending to pick it up, he toppled facedown to the ground.

His companions laughed, and the man with the handlebar mustache stepped up. He carried a big stick.

"Hey! Wait your turn," Baldy said. He pulled a small knife from his pocket, kissed it, and let it fly. It somersaulted three times and stuck in the toe of her father's right boot.

Her father grunted.

"Nice throw, you win." The mustache man passed his whiskey bottle to the bald man. "I say we change games. It's my turn, and I choose Stick and Ball." He hefted a smooth, hand-sized stone, tossed it in the air, and smacked it with his stick.

It flew faster than he could have thrown it, and hit her father dead center in the stomach. Father's eyes popped open.

Hudson clenched her fists in rage.

She glanced at the river bar to see how many in the mob were still standing. At least a dozen lay slumped against rocks, heads lolling, mouths open and snoring.

Red Duncan got to his feet. He raised his gun and fired off three shotgun blasts, jerking the crowd awake. Then, he tapped the side of his nose.

"Gather round. It's time for the verdict. Miles Taylor is about to be sentenced."

TWENTY-FOUR

Hudson realized she'd come too late. It was over. Duncan would have Father hauled onto the bar for execution.

However, the crowd yelled, "Speech! Speech! Speech!"

Red Duncan waved them to quiet down, but they continued to yell.

Then, to her amazement, the three guards quit their evil game and left their post, heading to join them. Was Lady Luck finally on her side?

Wait.

She'd chosen a terrible hiding spot. They were walking straight toward her! She lay flat and squeezed her eyes shut as if that would keep them from seeing her.

Boots scratched the ground less than two feet away. Hud waited to be hauled up by her suspenders. The four pairs of boots kept going. They'd missed her.

Rising, she stealthily crept toward her father—one bush, rock, and tree at a time. She kept one eye on the rowdy crowd, hoping they were too riled up to notice her.

Down on the river bar, Duncan motioned the men into silence.

"Let the trial begin!" He tapped his chin and made a show of looking thoughtful. Then, he grinned. "After a long consideration of the facts, I find Miles Taylor—" Duncan pointed his shotgun into the crowd before raising and aiming it at her father.

In the shadows, Hudson went stock still and waited for the blast

The miners scattered, tripping and falling over each other.

Duncan laughed loud and long. "It's not execution time. Yet. I have to list his crimes." He drank more whiskey and wiped his mouth with the back of his hand.

The miners had settled down, all eyes on Duncan.

She started to crawl.

Duncan raised a finger. "Count number one, I find Miles Taylor guilty of colluding with the enemy."

Cheers from the men. Several shots rang out.

Duncan's second finger went up. "Count number two, I find Miles Taylor guilty of murder."

More whoops and cheers.

"Lynch him!" shouted someone in the crowd. Soon they were all chanting together. "Lynch him!"

Duncan raised the shotgun overhead in both hands, punching the sky in time with the chants. "Lynch him! Lynch him!"

For the moment, they seemed more interested in chanting and grinning at one another than attacking. But that wouldn't last long.

Hudson crept into position behind the oak tree.

"Father. I'm here."

"Hud?" His shocked voice was weak—barely loud as a whisper. "You shouldn't be here. Ned promised he'd get you to safety."

"Lynch him! Lynch him! Lynch him!"

Hudson ran her hands over the rope and felt for the knot. "I'm going to cut you free. Keep standing until I'm finished."

"Lynch him! Lynch him! Lynch him!"

"You need to leave," Father said. "I can barely stand. Let alone walk."

"Please just try." She reached in her pocket and pulled out Ned's obsidian knife. "When I cut you loose, try not to fall."

"I can't run." He gasped out his words. "I'll slow you down. Get away. While you can."

"Lynch him! Lynch him! Lynch him!"

All of a sudden, the crowd silenced.

Uh oh. Were they coming? She didn't dare look.

She hurried, fumbling with the knife. It slipped from her grasp. She heard a chink, like the sound of breaking glass. *No. Not Ned's obsidian knife. Not now.* God, *why aren't you helping me?*

Maybe it only broke in two. She dropped to her knees and felt around but only came up with shards.

Red Duncan's voice roared. "Count number three, I find Miles Taylor guilty of stealing another man's gold."

"WAHOO!" The wild shouts resumed, louder than before. It seemed to go on and on forever.

"I'm sorry, Father," Hudson said, fumbling with the knot. "I broke the knife. It'll just take a little longer."

"No. You must escape," he said. "I'm sorry I wasn't a better father. I love you. Now go."

"I love you, too. And I'm not leaving without you."

"You're more stubborn than your aunt Gertrude."

"I learned from the best. Now try to stand taller and push your back against the tree trunk. It might put a little slack in the rope. Enough to loosen it so I can untie the knot."

He groaned and began to pant. "Does that help?"

"A little."

It didn't, but she wouldn't admit it. Not to him or herself. Panic settled in. She pulled and pushed at the knot. Refusing to give up. Refusing to leave her father for target practice. Refusing to let Red Duncan commit murder in the name of fake justice.

Wait. She stopped her struggles. The bald guard's knife had stuck in her father's boot.

"Can you see a knife in your right boot?"

"No. But I feel it. It's poking my big toe."

"Good. You be my eyes. Let me know if anyone's looking this way."

"Not directly."

"Good."

Hudson broke off a handful of leafy brush. Using it to camouflage her head and arms, she scooted just far enough to reach the boot with her left hand.

"I've got it," she said. "I'm going to pull it out."

"Do it quick."

"Okay. Three. Two. One." Hudson pulled, and the knife slid free. He sucked in a breath as she wriggled backward.

"Don't move," Father muttered. "Someone's looking."

Hudson held her breath and willed every cell to freeze. She waited.

"Clear," Father said.

Hudson scooted to safety and resumed sawing at the rope. "Get ready," she said. "I'm just about through."

Hudson felt warm breath on her neck and almost screamed. She spun, knife in hand, and came face-to-face with a big hairy nose.

"Chewed Ear," she whispered as the mule nuzzled her neck. Stunned, all she could thing was, perfect timing.

Then she noticed Ned. Against all odds, he'd actually managed it; he'd tracked down Chewed Ear. Not only that, but he'd followed her instructions to the letter: he was dressed like a miner—from the boots to the slouch hat. If they were spotted, he'd blend in.

"I'm glad I saw Chewed Ear first," she whispered. "The way you look, I might have hurt you."

"Or not," he said.

"You look even more convincing than I imagined." She turned to finish cutting the rope. "Did you set the fires?"

In answer, he glanced toward the miner's camp.

Red Duncan was the first to smell the smoke. He spun to stare at the tent village, his mean face frozen in horror.

Flames licked up the nearest canvas flaps.

"We're under attack!" Red Duncan screamed, his voice laced with fear. "The Indians, they've come for us. We're under attack!"

All chaos broke loose.

"Father, we're ready. Ned's disguised, so don't get excited when you see him. It will help us escape without being noticed. I'm going to make the final cut on the rope. He'll be there if you need help standing."

"And walking?" She heard the smile in her father's voice. "I suppose you have a solution for that, too."

"You'll only need to take a few steps. Chewed Ear will do the rest. Ready?"

"Do I have a choice?" her father replied.

"No. You're stuck with me."

Hudson made the final cut, and the rope dropped to the ground. Ned half-carried her father into the forest and helped settle him onto the mule. She climbed on behind him and wrapped her arms around him to hold him in place.

"No more talking until we're long gone," Hudson said.

She nudged the mule's flank, and Chewed Ear moved forward. Her father leaned against her, and she held him tight.

The plan was to head into the mountains, to ride the ridge before dropping back down to the main trail where Jason waited.

She still had no idea how they'd transport her injured father and Jason with his broken leg using a single donkey.

She startled when a second mule brayed behind her. It was black and marked with brutal scars. "It looks like Ned Duncan's poor mule! Ned, where did he come from?"

Ned didn't answer. "Hurry, we must go."

Why had Ned stolen it? It gave Duncan one more reason to come after them. Behind them, the fire burned higher and the shouts more frantic. Men were desperately trying to salvage their possessions and, no doubt, their gold.

Ned climbed onto Blackie's back and clicked his tongue. Soon they were riding side-by-side up a wide ravine.

Once out of voice range, Hudson demanded answers.

"Why did you steal Duncan's mule? That wasn't part of the plan. He'll be furious."

"One old mule will not add much to his anger."

"But then we're just as bad as he is. Taking what doesn't belong to us." She could feel her father tense.

Ned shook his head. "I did not take Blackie."

"You're riding him. Explain that."

"Chewed Ear made a new friend. Blackie followed us." Ned stroked the mule's neck. "I could not stop it."

"Seems to me," Father said, sounding a little stronger. "We're not the only ones wanting to escape Red Duncan."

Hudson smiled and hugged her father a little tighter. If he could joke, she knew he'd be okay. "Let's pick up the pace. We have a lot of miles to put between Red Duncan and us before daybreak."

TWENTY-FIVE

Three days later, Hudson sat on a log and watched Ned. He held a deer horn in one hand and an obsidian shard in the other. Volcanic glass chips formed a pile at his feet.

It was early morning. The sky was blue. The air fresh. The trees green. Her father had grown stronger with each passing day. He was almost back to normal.

Best of all, there had been no sign of Red Duncan or his men.

Nearby, Chewed Ear and Blackie lapped water from the clear stream. They'd made camp for the night behind a stand of young pepperwood. The trees gave off a sweet, spicy scent that reminded Hudson of Aunt Gertrude's kitchen.

"I'm sorry I broke your knife," she told Ned. "I wish *I* could make you a new one. Can you teach me?"

"Knapping is for boys and men." He was grinning but kept his eyes on his work. "Gathering roots and nuts is for women and girls. Like you."

She crossed her arms, her mouth hanging open. "How did you know?"

He kept grinning.

She said, "And by the way, I can do anything a boy can do, and better."

He laughed.

"Quit laughing. You better not tell anyone, I promised Father."

"Do not worry. Your secret is safe with me."

"What gave me away?"

"I knew from the first." He looked up. "Because you chatter and laugh like my sister. You remind me of her."

"Is Kachakaâch her name?"

He laughed again. "No. I believe it is your spirit animal. The bluebird that chatters all day to anyone who will listen."

"Hey! I am *not* a chatterbox!"

"A box? I did not say you were a box. I said, you are like a bird. A pretty bird the color of the ocean on a beautiful sunny day. I will miss your bird song."

"Oh." Hudson's face grew hot, and she hoped Ned hadn't noticed. Awkwardly, she said. "Aren't you coming with us?" When the words were out, she knew she wished he was.

He toyed with his knife and finally sighed. "No. I must return to my people downriver. It is where I belong."

"Hudson," her father called.

She jerked upright, pulled from the moment. "Yes?"

"Come over here. Jason has something to say to you."

Hudson rose, brushed off her pants, and joined them.

Jason faced her, hands fidgeting. In a rapid burst, he said, "I'm sorry for everything, I really am. I only did it because Red was going to kill me—he swore he would. No one's ever beat him, no one except you. You're smaller, but you're a better boy than me. You rescued your father from all those miners. And even though I was mean to you, you rescued me." Finally, he caught his breath and offered a trembling hand. "Truce?"

It was a big fancy speech, but could she believe him? She wanted to, and he did look sorry. She scuffed her feet in the dirt. What if Red Duncan had been her guardian? Fear was a powerful thing. Jason had been trying to survive. It's not what she would have done. When push came to shove, she would have run away.

She held out her hand. Jason took it and pumped her arm up and down.

"I forgive you, Jason," she said and meant it.

"I'm sorry about everything."

"No more apologies. We're good."

Hudson was uncertain about her future, but at least she wouldn't have to carry on being angry with Jason. It felt like dropping a heavy weight from her shoulders.

Now only one burden remained. Would her father let her stay with him? Or would her dream of being a family slip away?

Twenty-Six

Hudson and the others broke camp and continued on their trek.

Hudson's father broke the silence, "I'm still planning to go see Redick McKee, and maybe even the governor himself. He needs to hear about Red Duncan's attacks."

Hudson nodded. "I know. It's the only way to stop Red Duncan from hurting more people."

Still, she couldn't shake the dread that her father would send her back to Aunt Gertrude. After all, she'd cost him his place on the river. They were destitute. He didn't even have two buckets to his name.

Then her eyes brightened.

The nugget!

She had forgotten all about the nugget in her pocket.

After carrying it for so many days, the lump felt like a normal part of her clothes.

"Dad, I need to tell you something."

"What's wrong?"

She pulled out the gleaming lump and held it in her palm. The gold glinted in the sun.

"Eureka!" he gasped.

"I tried to tell you, before, when it all started. But then you got hurt and . . . I forgot." She sighed. "I'm not sure how I feel about all the trouble it's caused. Maybe, though . . ." She raised her eyes to his. "Maybe it's worth enough for us to make a new start?"

Her father was speechless. Was he angry?

"It's for you," she whispered.

"A lucky strike for us at last." He dropped down on one knee and squeezed her shoulders. "Hud, I'm proud of you. You've saved my life twice and now once again. All I've ever wanted was to make a life for us, to make enough to come back and get you and be a family."

"You . . . are you saying . . ."

"I'm saying that you've done what I couldn't." His eyes grew damp. "We're free. You've found us the riches to live a good life."

Her heart lurched. Was he saying what she hoped he was? "We? As in you and me? Together?"

He nodded and scooped her into a hug.

"Father, I love you," she said and hugged him back. "I promise to never let you down. Take the nugget, it's yours."

"No. You keep it for now," Father said, releasing her. "We'll cash it in and buy us a store. What do you think? Is that a plan?"

"It's a wonderful plan. What about Aunt Gertrude, what will you tell her?"

"That it's time I took care of my own."

Ned approached. "Where will you go?" he asked Jason.

Jason frowned. "I don't know. I don't have any family."

Father hesitated. Hudson had a terrible feeling he'd offer to let Jason join their newly-forged family. She might have forgiven Jason, but that would be awful. She'd never truly trust him.

Father cleared his throat. "My sister Gertrude in San Francisco will take you in. She is not an easy woman to live with, but I think you could manage it."

Hudson opened her mouth, surprised. Then again, Father was right. Jason was a big guy. Aunt Gertrude wouldn't dare take the whip to him. Instead, she'd put him to work running deliveries, she'd make sure he learned his manners, and with all her contacts, she might even find him a good job.

"That's an idea," Hudson said.

"Thank you," Jason said.

Her father settled his hand on the boy's shoulder. "Son, I suspect you might both be a benefit to one another."

Jason beamed.

Ned said, "It has all worked out well."

Hudson laughed and hugged her father. "We did it," she told him. "I can hardly believe it. I feel invincible. We found each other. We beat the odds. We escaped Red Duncan. We escaped the Gold Rush Massacre!"

The End

10 Fast Facts About the California Gold Rush

1. When the first miners arrived on the Klamath, the Karuk acted as helpful guides.
2. The Karuk lived in short, wooden houses built over underground basements, not in teepees.
3. The Karuk's friendliness faded when droves of miners arrived from all over the world and took control of the Klamath River.
4. Tensions exploded when some miners' cows ate poisonous Klamath weeds and died.
5. The miners claimed the Indians killed their cattle and burned Karuk villages in retaliation.
6. The surviving Karuk fled to the mountains.
7. According to history, local American militias were overly violent in taking revenge on natives for "crimes" the Indians supposedly committed.
8. Government official Redick McKee wrote to the governor of California, reporting that miners had murdered 30 or 40 innocent Karuk.
9. Prospecting gold was a gambler's life. Many got rich. Many went broke.
10. There is still gold to be found in California

California Gold Rush Quotes

The whole country . . . resounds with the cry of 'gold, GOLD, GOLD!' while the field is left half planted, the house half built, and everything neglected but the manufacture of shovels and pickaxes.

— From a contemporary newspaper

". . . the glimpse of something shining in the ditch. I reached my hand down and picked it up; it made my heart thump, for I was certain it was gold."

— James Wilson Marshall

"It appeared only an easier way of making a living for a few of us."

— *Adam Wicks, a gold prospector*

The rush to California . . . reflect the greatest disgrace on mankind. That so many are ready to live by luck, and so get the means of commanding the labor of others less lucky, without contributing any value to society!

— *Henry David Thoreau*

Talk like a Gold Miner!

WORDS MINED FROM THE GOLD RUSH

Paydirt: Gold miners called dirt that was full of gold paydirt. Today paydirt means something is financially beneficial.

Panned Out: If a pan was filled with gold, it panned out. Today panned out means something worked out well.

Eureka: An expression like WOW! that a miner said or shouted when he found gold. Today, it can mean 'I've found it.' Eureka is California's State motto. It's also a city in California's Gold Rush region.

Lucky Strike: Means that a miner found gold. Today it means a person has had a streak of good luck.

Forty-Niners: The nickname given to the 300,000 migrants who came to California to find gold. They were named "forty-niners" because they began to arrive in 1849. Today the 49ers are a football team in San Francisco. They've had gold rush luck because they've been to the super bowl seven times and have won five times.

Motherload / Mother Lode: A motherload is a large vein of gold or gold ore that's worth a lot of money. Today if you hit the motherload, you've hit a jackpot of great value.

Did You Know?

THE CALIFORNIA GOLD RUSH

Gold was first discovered in California at Sutter's fort in 1848. The following year gold was found in the Klamath and Trinity rivers in northern California.

Can you imagine wading in a river, looking down, and seeing gold at your feet? That's how it happened!

AMERICA'S FIRST GOLD RUSH

Here's something you might not know: America's first gold rush happened on the east coast. 50 years before the California Gold Rush began, prospectors discovered gold in Cabarrus County, North Carolina. The state even minted a coin to commemorate their gold rush.

MINERS CAME FROM ALL OVER THE WORLD

California's first miners came from Oregon, Mexico, and the Sandwich Islands (present-day Hawaii).

In the beginning, finding gold was pretty easy pickings. It was still plentiful, and there were fewer miners to share it.

Those first arrivers got a real jump on the thousands of people who came later--from Europe, Australia, China, and Latin America. By then, claims had been staked, the easy pickings were gone, and mining was just plum hard work. Still, if you were one of the lucky ones, you got rich. And that kept people coming.

At the height of the gold rush, 13 prospectors died while crossing a desert valley in eastern California. After the incident, the area received its name: *Death Valley,* which is still used today.

WHO GOT RICH?

Most would-be miners lost money during the Gold Rush, but the people who sold them picks, shovels, tents, and supplies became rich.

With so much gold available, basic supplies became expensive. A single egg could cost $25 in today's money, a cup of coffee went for more than $100, and replacing a pair of worn-out boots could set you back more than $2,500.

Samuel Brannan, a *shopkeeper and newspaper publisher,* was considered the wealthiest man in California during the Gold Rush.

Another Gold Rush success was Levi Strauss, who made and sold heavy-duty work pants to miners called (drum roll please) *jeans.* At first, the pants were made of thick canvas. They were hard to sew and probably uncomfortable to work in. He switched to blue denim, and the rest is history.

WHO LOST THE MOST?

The Klamath River is home to three main Indian tribes—the Karuk (pronounced Ka-rook), the Hupa (pronounced Hoopa), and the Yurok (pronounced Your rock).

The Klamath River was the lifeblood of the Native Americans, who relied on its salmon and trout for food. Klamath comes from the Indian word "Tlamatl," which means "swiftness."

Local Native Americans depended on traditional hunting, gathering, and agriculture. The arrival of the miners changed everything. With more arriving every month, it probably felt like an invasion.

The miners blocked the Karuk from accessing their land since they got in the way of gold extraction. The natives were told to "move on." Villages and sacred ceremonial spaces were replaced with mining camps.

The miners dammed the Klamath and diverted water for mining purposes. This destroyed habitats for fish and game.

Sadly, after only three short years, over half of the Karuk tribe had died from disease, starvation, or murder.

EFFECTS OF THE GOLD RUSH

The Gold Rush affected San Francisco, too. Beginning in 1848, it took just 4 short years for San Francisco to grow from about 200 residents to over 36,000!

Once settled, it kept growing. Its population in 2021 is 883,255.

By the time the Gold Rush ended, California had gone from a thinly populated ex-Mexican territory to a state.

Reportedly, almost 92% of the people prospecting for gold were men.

Agriculture and ranching expanded throughout the state to meet the needs of the settlers.

With so many miners, the easy picking soon dwindled. Americans began to drive out foreigners. After two years of mass immigration, the new California State Legislature levied a foreign miners' tax of $20/month ($600 per month as of 2019).

New methods of transportation developed as steamships came into regular service.

By 1869, railroads were built from California to the eastern United States.

GOLD MINING TECHNIQUES

Gold Panning

Early miners simply panned for gold using a large metal pan along rivers and streams. Panning cannot be done on a large scale. Try your hand at gold panning using the activity in the next section.

Diverting the river

Miners build dams and channels for easy access to the riverbed.

Sluice boxes (cradles, rockers, and long-toms)

These were developed to process larger volumes of gravel. They separated the gold from dirt using water and movement. How? Gold is heavy and settles to the bottom.

Hydraulic mining

Miners aim a high-pressure water stream at gold-bearing gravel beds on hillsides above the rivers or streams.

Dredging

Developed in the late 1890s, dredging allowed miners to dig and process large quantities of gravel at one time.

Hard-rock mining

Miners blast gold veins from 'host rocks' containing gold (usually quartz). These host rocks are brought to the surface and crushed. The gold is then leached from the crushed rock with arsenic or mercury. Unfortunately, this method causes extensive environmental damage. The hard-rock mining technique produced the most gold from California's Mother Lode.

TRY YOUR HAND AT MINING WITH THIS GOLD PANNING ACTIVITY

** Recommended as an outdoor activity*

MATERIALS

Quantities will depend on the number of kids participating.

- metal pie tins (*Marie Callender pie tins work the best*)
- a mixture of dirt, sand, and gravel
- small garden hand trowel
- 2 large tubs
- 1 small bottle or zip-lock bag to keep the *gold* participants find
- a scale (*to weigh the gold participants find*)
- 'gold' - using one of the suggestions below

GOLD OPTIONS:

- Iron Pyrite, a.k.a. *fools gold*
- Paint pea gravel with metallic gold-colored paint

SET UP YOUR GOLD FIELD

1. Chose a workable and safe location.
2. In one tub, mix your "gold", dirt, sand, and gravel.
3. Fill the second tub with water. You might want to have a garden hose ready to refill the tub if necessary.

THE TECHNIQUE

(*If doing this as a group activity, you may want to practice this before you gather up your group.*)

1. Using a garden trowel, shovel "pay dirt" into a pie tin.
2. Dip the edge of your pan of dirt into the water and fill it WITH JUST ENOUGH WATER TO BE ABLE TO SWIRL THE DIRT. Don't spill the dirt mixture into the tub. KEEP YOUR WATER CLEAN.

3. HOLDING YOUR PAN WITH BOTH HANDS, step away from the water tub and squat over your pan.
4. Shake your pie tin pan until the water looks dirty. You can also use ONE hand to stir up the dirt.
5. Carefully tip out the dirty water without losing any rocks.
6. Pick out any large rocks that aren't "gold."
7. Add fresh water and repeat. Do this as many times as it takes to wash the dirt away and the water is clean.
8. Once the water is clean, squat over the water tub and rotate the pan in a circular motion, letting the gravel bits dribble into the water. As soon as you spot a "gold nugget" in the pan, remove it and place it in a bottle or zip-lock.
9. Continue to pan until your pan is empty.

GATHER YOUR GOLD MINERS AND START MINING

1. Begin by demonstrating how to pan for gold.
2. Give each child a pie tin and bag or bottle for their gold.
3. One at a time, let participants fill their pan from the "pay dirt" pile. Don't let them try to find the gold in the tub. To avoid this happening, an adult or assigned group leader can fill their pans.
4. Let participants pan, giving advice when needed.
5. The number of kids that can pan at one time will depend on the size of your gold field.
6. At the end of the activity, each child weighs their gold.
7. BONUS IDEAS: Turn this into a math activity. Based on the week's current gold price, figure out how much their "gold" would be worth if it was real. You could also set up a "store" where they could buy things with their gold.

Thank you

We hope you enjoyed this book, Dear Reader!
We're always hard at work crafting stories with you in mind.
Please consider giving this book some stars using Amazon's star feature. Your feedback means the world to us!

~ SD Brown and Scott Peters

THE I ESCAPED SERIES

I Escaped North Korea!

I Escaped The California Camp Fire

I Escaped The World's Deadliest Shark Attack

I Escaped Amazon River Pirates

I Escaped The Donner Party

I Escaped The Salem Witch Trials

I Escaped Pirates In The Caribbean

I Escaped The Tower of London

I Escaped Egypt's Deadliest Train Disaster

Also by SD Brown

Code Orange Cancun

Escape To Molokai

Also by Scott Peters

Mystery of the Egyptian Scroll

Mystery of the Egyptian Mummy

Join the I Escaped Club

Get a free pack of mazes and word finds to print and play!

https://www.subscribepage.com/escapedclub

Made in the USA
Las Vegas, NV
12 March 2024